THE HOLIDAY
DETOUR

Visit us at www.boldstrokesbooks.com

THE HOLIDAY DETOUR

by
Jane Kolven

2020

CREDITS
EDITOR: CINDY CRESAP
PRODUCTION DESIGN: SUSAN RAMUNDO
COVER DESIGN BY TAMMY SEIDICK

Dedication

For Lizzi, who picked me up in their rusty car
and has been changing my world ever since.

CHAPTER ONE

Among the things I disliked most in the world were long car rides, and yet every year I found myself putting off booking a flight home to the suburbs of Chicago until it was too late, the tickets were all too expensive (if there were even any left), and voilà. I would be stuck driving all the way from Cleveland in the frigid, dark winter by myself with nothing to do in the car but listen to the Christmas music that had taken over every radio station.

Why did I do this every year if I hated it so much? My nana. I didn't have many friends left in Highland Park, Illinois, where I grew up, but my grandmother still lived there. I invited her to celebrate Christmas with me in Cleveland, but at eighty-five she was better off staying put. At thirty-two, I could much more easily go to her, even if I had to listen to "The Most Wonderful Time of the Year" on repeat across three states.

The more the singer emphasized how wonderful it was, the more I was convinced it was actually lousy. This year promised to be even worse because Nana had called to tell me that Mitchell Wormerstein would also be home visiting his own grandmother, who happens to live a block away from Nana. Mitchell and I went to school together from kindergarten, when he picked his nose and ate what he found, to eighth grade, when he popped his zits in class and they squirted on his homework. In high school his family had thankfully moved away. Since it had been some fifteen years since I'd seen him, Nana thought I might like to visit with him. I would have rather given Nana a pedicure.

I hadn't even made it to Toledo when my phone rang with an unknown number. Since my friends always texted me like normal people, I was in the habit of assuming phone calls were from debt collectors for some bill I forgot to pay, which made me absolutely not want to answer the phone. But I was also in the habit of worrying that someone might be calling to tell me something bad had happened to Nana. Both possibilities made my heart skip a beat whenever the phone rang, for very different reasons, but because of the latter, I always answered, just in case.

"Hello, is this Dana?"

"Yes," I answered nervously.

"This is Mitch Stein," a suave voice said. He chuckled, and it was the sound a chocolate shaving on top of a cheesecake would make if it made sounds. "Actually, you knew me as Mitchell Wormerstein."

I nearly swerved off the highway.

"Mitchell? Mitch?" I repeated. Then psychotically, with way too much enthusiasm, I screamed into the phone, "Mitch! Hi! How are you?!"

"I'm doing fine." He cooed like a 1950s movie star whose hair was slicked back with Brilliantine, but Mitchell Wormerstein—Mitch Stein—had been a bug-eyed, chubby-cheeked freak when I'd last seen him. I wasn't fooled by a silken voice. "You're probably wondering how I got your number and why I'm calling."

No kidding.

"Your grandmother gave your number to my grandmother, and before you get angry at them—or me—I promise you I don't have any intention of bothering you about meeting up over Christmas."

Like many people, when I felt backed into a corner, I tended to do and say the exact opposite of what I was thinking and feeling. I heard myself give an artificial laugh and promise him, "Not at all, Mitch! I'd love to meet up while we're both in town! It'd be great after all these years!"

"Oh, well, okay, I think I can find some time for that." He sounded a little off-put.

I tightened my grip on the steering wheel. How dare he suggest he would be busier than I would and that he would deign to grant me some of his precious time? He'd once conned me into playing Uno in a corner of the classroom during indoor recess on a rainy day, and I'd only said yes because I didn't know how to say no. He'd spent the whole time farting and pretending it wasn't him.

"Anyway," Mitchell—*Mitch*—continued as if it wasn't supremely gracious of me to even be talking to someone so obviously lower than me in the elementary school social hierarchy, "the reason I'm calling is that my grandmother wanted to know if it would be okay if Mrs. Gottfried came over here tonight. Granny says Mrs. Gottfried is usually alone because you can't get here in time, so she wanted me to check with you about your travel plans. We obviously don't want to interfere in anything you might have going on, but we didn't want your grandmother to be alone."

That was sweet of his grandmother Ruthie. She and Nana had known each other since their first year of high school. They'd gone to separate colleges but stayed friends, and they had both moved from Rogers Park to Highland Park in the 1950s when they got married and started having kids. My dad had been the first born to the two families in 1957, and Ruthie's daughter Lila came shortly after. I think Nana had always expected them to end up together, and maybe giving Mitchell—*Mitch*—my phone number was her way of uniting the clans a generation later.

As if Nana didn't know I was gay.

"That's very thoughtful," I told Mitch. "You know Nana refuses to celebrate Christmas, right? She'll eat and drink your wine, but she'll get huffy if you try to make her do anything more than that."

Mitch gave a mirthful chuckle, and this time I thought of a powdery snowfall sprinkling down from the heavens. Had he actually grown up to be attractive, or did he just get a really good voice after puberty? The last time I'd spoken to him, he had sounded like a cat in heat.

"We actually do some Christmas stuff," he explained, "since my father never converted, and my mom says it's important to her that we share his heritage. But Granny will probably get her revenge by keeping the menorah out even though Hanukkah was two weeks ago. She and Mrs. Gottfried are welcome to spin dreidels if they'd like. Last year, when Granny visited us, she staged a murder scene with some reindeer figurines. She made us all act as detectives to figure out who killed it."

Ruthie was lucky her second daughter, Hannah, was still alive to torture her into celebrating Christmas. Like many families in Highland Park, mine was Jewish, and so, for the most part, was Mitch's. But unlike many families, mine was just my grandmother and me. My grandfather had died of cancer when I was four, and my parents had died in a car accident while I was in college. Nana and I had been surviving on our own ever since.

"Anyway," Mitch continued, "everyone will be there this year, Lila and my folks, me, Ruthie, and I think Franklin Silverman is coming. Your grandmother would be very welcome."

"Really, it's so nice of you to think of her," I repeated. "But I'm actually on my way to Illinois right now. I should be there by dinnertime unless a snowstorm kicks in. So Nana won't be alone."

I expected Mitch to conclude our conversation at that point, but instead he said quite insistently, "Oh, well, of course, you're more than welcome."

I lied and said I would be delighted to see him, and we hung up. I definitely did not want to celebrate Christmas among a big family, especially a semi-Jewish one that didn't even want to be celebrating Christmas, and I certainly did not want to be forced to interact with Mitchell Wormerstein. Mitch Stein. Whatever he called himself now. I groaned aloud in the car to no one, adjusted the heater, and angrily switched the radio station away from "Holly Jolly Christmas." The next station was playing "Jingle Bell Rock." Just great.

CHAPTER TWO

Somewhere in Indiana, I stopped to fill my gas tank and get something to eat. Although I was generally a healthy eater, I allowed myself to eat whatever I wanted on road trips. The problem with this was that Nana always wanted to feed me when I showed up on her doorstep, but by that point I was usually so bloated with soda and fries that I would nearly vomit at the mention of food. I supposed I was nearing the age when I should have started thinking more carefully about what I put into my body, but...Well, the slushy machine at the gas station had something lime green that was calling my name. It was on sale for seventy-nine cents, so after I went to the bathroom, I filled a cup, grabbed a package of Flamin' Hot Cheetos, and returned to my car, proud that my late lunch cost less than three dollars.

A few miles down the highway, I caught a glimpse of myself in the rearview mirror. There was electric red powder dotting my lips, and my tongue was slime green. For a moment I wondered if things like this explained why I was always single.

Sometimes on long trips I tried to imagine someone sitting in the passenger seat. I didn't know what she'd look like, what snacks she'd get from the gas station, or whether she'd sing off-key and loudly like me, at least when the radio stations weren't taken over by the Ronettes maniacally repeating the phrase "sleigh ride."

I was halfway to fantasizing about a cross-country road trip all the way from Maine to California, something I'd always wanted to do but had never done because I didn't want to go alone, when my check engine light came on. Before I could think about why or what to do about it, an alarm started dinging, and I frantically tried to steer to the nearest off-ramp.

I didn't make it.

My car made a horrible grinding noise a few yards from the off-ramp, a thunderous metallic clunk that rattled the whole car, and then the engine died. I put the gearshift in park, turned the ignition off and on, and tried to restart the engine. Nothing. The radio and lights didn't even come on.

I didn't know anything about cars. I had never hit a squirrel, I didn't know how to change my own oil, and I definitely couldn't take a peek under the hood to see what was going on. The one time I got a flat tire, I discovered it after coming out of Target with about three hundred dollars' worth of goods in plastic shopping bags. I'd called roadside assistance to come and fix it and hoped my frozen dinners wouldn't melt before they arrived. But I didn't need to be a mechanic to know that the metallic clunk I'd heard just now wasn't good. It sounded as if part of the engine had fallen out. Somehow I knew in the pit of my stomach that my sweet baby car, which had been a graduation present from Nana and which had been in my life for almost ten years since, was completely, truly dead.

I swore out loud.

It took me a few seconds of sitting behind the wheel while cars whizzed past me at seventy miles an hour to snap out of my shock. Then I took a deep breath and gathered my thoughts. The most important thing was to get out of the way of traffic before someone accidentally sideswiped me or killed us both. I tried the key in the ignition once more, but it was pointless. I briefly thought about getting out and pushing the car, but that would pose a much greater safety risk than leaving it where it was. No, I needed professional assistance.

I fumbled around for my phone, which I had carelessly tossed on the passenger seat after that unexpected phone call from Mitchell Wormerstein. It wasn't on the seat anymore, so I had to unbuckle my seat belt and lean across the console, feet coming off the ground, to peek under the passenger seat. I spied the hot pink case tucked against the metal track used to adjust the seat, grabbed it, and righted myself. The screen had some crumbs from God knows what on it, which I blew off. For good measure, I rubbed the screen on my jeans.

New problem: the phone wasn't charged. Talking to Mitchell Wormerstein must have depleted the battery, since I hadn't charged the phone the night before because I am a total screw-up. I had assumed it wouldn't be a problem because I could charge the phone while driving, but obviously that wasn't going to work now.

There was a whopping four percent left to the battery, and I was going to use it. Before I attempted to dial, I scrounged in the glovebox for the little folder in which I kept the insurance information. Once I'd located the number for roadside assistance, I dialed. I managed to get someone on the phone and tell them which highway I was on, but I didn't know where I was exactly. I was past the off-ramp sign, and I hadn't been paying a lot of attention before the car died. I was fumbling with the map app to figure out where the little blue dot was when the battery finally died, in the middle of my phone call for help.

Well, this was a promising start to the day.

My car was getting really cold.

I tapped my forehead against the steering wheel a few times, contemplating what would happen if I got out and tried to walk down the off-ramp for help. How far could I walk without getting hit by a car? How far would I have to walk in the cold before I found a store or a gas station? I remembered when there used to be pay phones in public places and wondered why we had been so quick to give them up.

My next thoughts were about Nana, who wouldn't worry if I were an hour or so behind schedule but who could have her own emergency and no way to reach me. I couldn't sit in the car all day hoping roadside assistance had actually gotten enough information to come for me. No, I'd have to venture out into the cold and hope for the best. My scarf and gloves were on the seat beside me. I bundled myself up and climbed out of the car, flattening myself against the driver's side door as a semi-truck came roaring by.

Those off-ramps to highways never looked very steep or very long to me when I was driving them, but on foot it took me a really long time to get to the bottom. I was only wearing Converse high-tops, and since I was too afraid of being hit by a car to walk in the road, my feet were soaking wet with snow slush. At the intersection, I slid on a patch of ice and landed hard on my bum. Things hurt, my pride most of all, but I managed to push myself onto all fours and then back to standing.

"This sucks." I tried to sniffle up the snot that was running down my upper lip. I felt like Mitchell Wormerstein.

A beat-up blue truck honked from the other side of the street. The driver rolled the window down, and someone with floppy brown chin-length hair leaned out. "Are you okay?"

Was I okay? Not in the least. I was most definitely not okay. But did I want to admit it to a stranger? I didn't know. From the little I could see of the person leaning out the truck window, I thought she was a woman, though with the haircut and voice it wasn't totally clear. She had giant brown eyes, a gorgeous elfish type, and she didn't match the truck at all.

"Do you need me to take you to the gas station?" the person yelled.

I waited for a car to pass through the intersection and then ran across the street with my hands warming in my pockets, trying not to think about how dorky I must have looked. I slowly approached the truck, feeling nervous and trying not to do that awkward shy-smile thing I usually did when I found someone attractive.

"Um...what?"

Best first line ever, Dana.

"What are you doing walking around the highway? Did you run out of gas?"

I shrugged and wiped my dripping nose with a gloved hand. "My car died, and then my phone died." I hadn't realized it until I tried to talk, but my mouth had frozen. My words came out in an indiscriminate slur.

"Did you just fall on your butt?"

"What? No." My bruised bottom protested at the injustice of it all.

"Sounds like you're having a rough day." Up close, the driver looked like a woman. She had the smooth skin and delicate features of a woman, anyway. She patted the truck door. "Hop in, and I'll take you to the gas station."

"I can walk just fine."

She rolled her eyes. "I'm not a serial killer."

"A serial killer wouldn't admit to being a serial killer."

"Suit yourself, the gas station is two miles back that way."
She jerked her thumb in the direction from which she'd come.
She started to roll the window up.

"Okay, take me!" I cringed, hearing how desperate I
sounded. *Take me, I'm yours! Take me now, I need it!* I'd just
met this person, and she was already hearing my sex screams.
"Um, could you...would you mind taking me? To the gas
station. In your truck."

"I can take you." She smirked. She totally smirked.

I couldn't blush in the cold, but I made some weird gasping
sound like a donkey. I tried to cover by coughing loudly. "My
asthma," I lied. "I'd really appreciate a ride because the cold
air isn't good for my asthma."

"Then don't just stand there. Get in."

I hurried around the back of the truck to the other side.
I stood at the passenger side door for a second trying to
figure out how to hoist myself up. The truck was so tall that I
had to use the hand on the door for leverage and vault myself
upward. I landed with an ungraceful plop on the bench
seat and then reached over to close the creaky, stiff door.
Once it was safely shut and locked, I leaned against it
and hoped I might fall back out to save myself from my
embarrassment.

I sneaked a look at the driver.

Her hair was a little shorter than her chin and fell in pieces
across her face. She was wearing a tan Carhartt jacket, the

kind I expected to see on a hunter, and it was at least two sizes too big for her tiny frame. I hadn't noticed whether the license plate on the truck was from Indiana, but I assumed so. She looked like a wild country animal.

"Where were you heading?" she asked, lowering the volume on the radio. It had been playing some kind of new agey music, not country.

"I'm going to Chicago. My grandmother lives in the suburbs, and I always spend Christmas with her."

"What happened to your car?"

I shrugged. "The check engine light came on, and then everything started dinging, and then there was a banging, like some metal thing punching some other metal thing, and then it just died."

"And your phone is dead?"

"Yeah, I forgot to charge it."

"That was a pretty stupid thing to do in the winter when you're driving alone on the interstate in the middle of nowhere."

I blinked a few times. "Yes, it was." Not that I needed someone else to chastise me.

A minute later, we pulled up to a ramshackle gas station, and she put the truck in park. Then she actually turned the engine off. I must have made a face of surprise because she explained, "I'll come in and wait in case you need me to take you back to your car."

"Um…okay." I eased the truck door open and slid out, but I managed to land on my feet. It took a lot of strength to get the door shut again.

Inside the gas station, my rescuer hovered by the magazine rack while I explained to the man behind the counter what had happened to my car. He yelled over my shoulder for someone in the back of the store, and a man in coveralls with a patch that said "Sam" came out. He offered to tow the car to the station for a hundred bucks, but he said fixing the car would probably take a while, this close to Christmas.

"You're not going to be fixing it," my driver interrupted. "Don't get her hopes up."

They argued for a little bit, but I didn't really understand what they were talking about. I wondered if my roadside assistance call had succeeded. Maybe there was a perfectly normal tow truck driver waiting by my car, wondering where I was, and I was a few miles away without a phone, dependent on some pixie-sized person who was telling off "Sam."

Sam rubbed his hands against the front of his coveralls and looked at me sheepishly. "Truth is, ma'am, your car probably needs a whole new engine, if it can even be repaired. But depending on how old it is and what the make and model are, repairing it might cost more than it's worth. You're probably looking at salvage."

Salvage. They wanted to salvage my beautiful baby, the first car I had ever owned. That car had taken me from my first year out of college to my new job in Cleveland. It had carried me between Chicago and Cleveland faithfully for a decade. Maybe I had neglected to get oil changes as frequently as I should have, but I had loved it and washed it and replaced the muffler one winter after it had rusted out. The car was entirely paid for, and now that I had quit my job, there was no way I could buy another one. I wasn't "credit-worthy," and I definitely didn't have any money in savings for a down payment. That car owed it to me not to leave me stranded in rural Indiana on Christmas Eve.

Unexpectedly, my eyes welled up, and I blinked back hot tears before I started crying over a car in front of these strangers. The driver put her arm around me. Her canvas jacket made scratchy sounds. Its bulk was deceptive, making her look older and bigger than she probably was. And tougher than she apparently was. Her kindness touched me, and the tears fell freely.

"Hey," she soothed, "it's okay. We'll make sure you get to your grandma. You won't miss Christmas with her."

Chapter Three

A waitress set a piece of cherry pie in front of me and topped off the white ceramic mug of weak but hot coffee. She slapped a paper check face-down on the table and scooted off. My phone was plugged into an outlet underneath the table, and I checked it again to see how much battery power it had now. Since my car was officially toast, I needed to figure out where the nearest rental service was and then figure out how to get there. I highly doubted I could find a cab, licensed or otherwise, in whatever small town I happened to be in.

Sam had promised to store the car free of charge until after the holidays to give me a chance to figure out what I wanted to do with it. He'd driven out to the highway and towed it back. I'd paid him and thrown in a new phone charger, and my blue truck savior had deposited me at this little diner down the road from the gas station before wishing me luck and heading on her merry way.

"All right, Dana," I muttered to myself, "let's get organized." First, I needed to tell Nana what was going on, so she didn't worry. I called her. I told her the car had "a little problem" and that I would be arriving much later than I had anticipated. Then I pulled up my recent incoming calls and found Mitchell Wormerstein's number. I explained the situation in more detail and asked if he'd mind checking in on Nana. He promised it wouldn't be any trouble.

"But don't tell her what's actually happening," I added.

"Okay."

His voice sounded puzzled, and I didn't want him to doubt that I was a good granddaughter. "I didn't tell her my car is dead-dead," I explained, "so she doesn't worry about my safety and stuff. I just told her it had some mechanical problems."

"Okay."

I really didn't need Mitchell Wormerstein—*Mitch Stein*—making me feel guilty about telling a white lie to an eighty-five-year-old in order to spare her worry. What did he know about taking care of a grandmother from a distance? He didn't know anything about the way I had to always check in on her and how she was the only person in my life I could trust unfailingly but how I still had to shield her from certain things, such as the fact that I had quit my job without any money in savings like a total moron. Or that the car she had bought me was now going to be scrapped for parts, and I wasn't going to have any way to get around, and I was stuck in Nowhere, Indiana, on Christmas Eve and two seconds away from crying because this situation completely sucked.

What did Mitchell know about any of that?

"Your discretion is appreciated," I said tartly.

Maybe my tone of voice registered to him, or maybe I'd misinterpreted his "okays," but the suave phone sex operator voice returned. "Hey, Dana," he purred, "I get it. We'll make sure she has a good night and doesn't worry. But you be careful out there, okay?"

I thanked him and set about my next task, which was figuring out how I was going to get mobile again. The internet signal in the diner was really weak, and I was struggling to get a search for car rental services to load and cursing. My cherry pie sat in front of me, taunting me. I just wanted to eat in peace, but I had to figure out my next move.

The search screen came back with a note that there was no internet signal. I swore.

The door to the diner jingled as it opened, jingling the stupid sleigh bells tied to the hinge. The truck driver who'd rescued me came back in, mirrored sunglasses covering her face. She slid them up to her head, glanced around, and nodded in satisfaction when she spotted me.

Without asking, she slid into the booth across from me. "How's it going?"

I looked around, but no one else in the diner was paying attention to us. "What are you doing here? I thought you left."

She shrugged. "I was worried about you, so I thought I'd check to see how it's going." She picked up my fork and ate a piece of my cherry pie.

I gaped. "I can't believe you just ate my pie!"

"I just spent an hour helping you. You can spare me a piece of pie."

"I would have offered if you had given me a chance. But you dumped me here and ran away, and now you're back and just help yourself without asking? What is wrong with you?"

She took a drink of my coffee. A big drink. Considering it was still steaming, I could imagine how seared her throat must be. She waved to the waitress to refill the mug.

"Who do you think you are?" I asked crisply.

"I'm Charlie."

My eyes narrowed. "You know what I mean."

"What's your name, anyway?"

"Dana."

"Dana, I have a proposition for you, but I don't want you to be freaked out."

My mind went to dirty places at the word "proposition," and then I got annoyed at myself because why would I think about having sex with someone who abandoned people in the middle of nowhere and then stole their pie?

"My family actually lives in Deerfield, and I was headed there tomorrow."

Deerfield was another northern suburb of Chicago, a few minutes to the west of Highland Park, where Nana lived. It seemed like a very strange coincidence, one that was probably totally fictional and that would result in me being in forty-five pieces buried in the woods.

But then again, Charlie had made a point of coming back to the diner to check on me. To tell the truth, I had been disappointed when she'd left, but I figured I should have been grateful for any help she'd been willing to give me. After Sam had towed my car, she had suggested getting some coffee to warm up, and I had greedily said yes. But once we pulled up to the diner, I felt guilty at putting her out. I had thanked her and jumped out of the truck, insistent that she had already done too much for me. It hadn't occurred to me until that moment that maybe she had meant getting coffee together.

Had she come back to check on me because she was equally disappointed at driving off and leaving me?

Now she was forking down my cherry pie and coffee refill, which I supposed I owed her for helping me, but sheesh, she could have at least waited until I'd offered it or ordered a second piece for her. She was infuriating in an electrifying, dangerous but desirable way. The thought of spending hours in the truck with her, driving the remaining swath of Indiana…

"Would you like to drive together?" she asked, in case I'd missed her earlier hinting. "I was planning to leave tomorrow, but if you're willing to come to my house now, I can pack pretty quickly, and we can hit the road again soon. You'd only be a few hours behind schedule."

I felt hot all over. I couldn't answer.

Charlie presumed my silence was an offer for more pie. She slid the whole plate to her side of the table. "If it's not too creepy," she added between bites.

I found Charlie's attitude rude but mostly alluring. There was something about her confidence and swagger that threw me off balance. She had rescued me in a moment at which I did not know what to do. She had let me cry on her shoulder at the gas station, and she had made some of the important decisions for me when I felt incapacitated to make them myself. Not that I'm especially femme or weak, but sometimes it's nice to be taken care of. I also liked that she was that strong and confident even though she looked twenty and weighed eighty pounds.

I had another thought. "Your family is in Deerfield?" This was completely incongruous with what I'd seen of Charlie so far. Deerfield is another one of the suburbs heavily populated with Jewish families, though not quite as many as Highland Park, and more affluent than the average neighborhood, though again not quite as wealthy as Highland Park. Still, Deerfield wasn't a random stretch of suburbs. Charlie drove a truck that had rust spots and lived in rural Indiana. Nothing about her said she came from hoity-toity North Shore stock. "What are you doing here?"

"Here where?"

"Here in…wherever we are."

"The same as you, driving home for the holidays."

"Where do you live?"

"Goshen."

I wasn't entirely sure where that was or how far it might be from where we were presently sitting. "I live in Cleveland," I volunteered. "I work at the art museum." Worked, technically, but my quit-before-they-fire-you recent separation was still so fresh that I supposed I could still claim it as a place of employment until my last paycheck was deposited into my checking account.

"I take care of pigs."

"You don't smell like pigs." My hand flew to my mouth. "I'm so sorry. I can't believe I said that."

Charlie grinned, creating the deepest dimples I'd ever seen in her round cheeks. "That's all right, it comes with the territory."

I still wasn't sure if committing to five hours in a car with a stranger was a good idea, but I'd had nothing but trouble with my car insurance company and the internet connection in the dinky town. Getting a ride wouldn't solve all my problems, since I'd still have to figure out a way back here to deal with junking the car and then figure out how to get home to Cleveland. But Charlie made me feel like I wanted to bury my head under the covers in embarrassment and like I wanted to stare at her all day. Both at the same time. Now that she had come back to the diner, I didn't want her to leave again.

"You'd really take me to Chicago?" I asked, in case she might have rescinded the offer in the few minutes I'd managed to insult her.

"It's not any trouble." She shrugged. "I'm going the same way, and it's always a really lonely drive." She beamed at me. "Do you like singing Christmas songs?"

All the charm went out of the moment, the flash of fantasy that had been forming in my head destroyed before I had even fully visualized it. "Sure," I lied, my voice betraying my words.

Charlie laughed. "I hate it, too. Let's pick out an audiobook before we hit the road."

The diner was attached to a little convenience store, which had a rack of popular crime fiction audiobook CDs on a spinning tower near the checkout. Charlie said she liked to listen to murder mysteries on long car rides to make the journey go faster and to avoid hitting spots where the radio was nothing but static or conspiracy talk radio. She failed to explain why she didn't just download them to her phone like a normal person. Instead, she picked out a bargain set of CDs with an image of a chalk body outline and some police tape on the cover. She told me she never paid more than ten dollars for an audiobook because she was only going to listen to it once and then give it away. This time, she didn't have to pay, as I jammed my credit card in the machine at the register before she could. I figured it was only fair, since she was doing a lot for me.

We got the audiobook package unwrapped and put the first CD in Charlie's radio, but we never even made it past, "This audiobook has been recorded by..." before we started talking.

Charlie had grown up in the Chicago area like me but had stayed for college. After graduating, she'd taken a job in food research for Kraft. A few years ago, a merger had put her out of work and ready to pursue a graduate degree to advance her career. She wanted to focus more on animal health and sustainability, so she'd come to Indiana.

"When you said you work with pigs, I thought you were a farmer," I confessed.

"I kind of am, in a way." Charlie shot me a side look. "But, no, I guess I don't raise pigs for slaughter. Does it change your opinion of me?"

Yes, to be honest. Maybe that made me a snob. I thought Charlie was a country bumpkin type, kind of sexy in how radically different her life was from mine, but nobody I could ever actually be involved with. I was the kind of person who refused to wear snow boots because they were ugly and always clashed with my outfits. I wore ballet flats to work in the winter and then changed into heels at the office. I'd never seen a pig up close.

"I don't know," I answered carefully. "Would it change your opinion of me if I said yes?"

Charlie contemplated this for a moment. "Dana Gottfried. Sounds like someone who likes to read books and bake cookies and has a vision board for her dream trip to the Galapagos Islands." I opened my mouth to respond, but she quickly amended, "Make that Tuscany."

I most certainly did not have a vision board for anything, especially not trips to Tuscany. Where, by the way, I had already been twice. "At least what I do doesn't hurt animals."

"You think I hurt animals?"

"Pig research?" I scoffed. So maybe Charlie wasn't a farmer slopping them or whatever, but didn't that mean she performed weird genetic splices on them and gave them measles to figure out if it would kill them? How disgusting.

"Yeah, pig research," she shot back. "I figure out what combination of foods will keep their immune systems the healthiest because no one seems to want to give up bacon any time soon, despite the fact that pigs are smarter than dogs."

"They are?"

"Yes. I love my pigs. I hate the thought of anyone hurting pigs."

I bit my lip. I was a champion bacon eater. "So are you a vegetarian?"

Charlie nodded. "Vegan mostly, except you know, sometimes, I really crave cherry pie." She winked lasciviously at me.

I laughed in spite of myself. "For the record, I don't have a vision board, and I've been to Tuscany already."

"Of course you have."

"I'm sorry if I was being a snob."

"I'm sorry I said you had a vision board—if that kind of thing upsets you. For the record, I don't think there's anything wrong with being proactive about your dreams."

Um, okay. "I don't bake either," I told her.

"Ah, yes, okay, so you're the type who gets a pastry for breakfast with her soy latte and always orders out."

She had me there. I didn't answer.

We sat in silence, letting the voice of the audiobook narrator fill the air although I couldn't tell what was going on in the story. I ruminated on Charlie's assumptions about me and my own preconceptions of her. She probably hated me for being some wimpy woman who couldn't take care of her car, I decided, and who was too dumb to charge her phone. She probably thought I wasn't cut out for the real world. She didn't know anything about me, about what I'd lived through and how tough I really was. How dare she judge me so quickly?

"I'm a lesbian," I blurted. I sucked in a breath and waited for her reaction.

A slow, devilish smile inched across Charlie's face, but her eyes never strayed from the road. "Darlin'," she drawled, "do you think you'd even be sittin' there if I didn't already know that?"

CHAPTER FOUR

I wanted to slide down the seat and into the floorboards. If my face could have gotten any hotter, we could have turned the heat off in the truck, and I could have served as a natural radiator. I hoped the truck would go over a bump, the door would pop open, and I'd fall out, rolling to safety in the drainage ditch along the highway, where I'd be conveniently rescued by my roadside assistance, who hadn't given up on me and who was going to be a nice, normal straight person in a nice, normal sedan.

"You going to be okay?"

Charlie knew she had me. That was even worse than blurting my sexuality like I had when I was what we called a "baby dyke" in college, desperate to find other lesbians for friendship or more. When I was nineteen, I had worked the fact that I had just come out into every conversation imaginable. In line at the cafeteria, I'd ask for a cheese pizza "for the newest member of the LGBT community." At parties, if someone handed me a drink, I'd ask if they were gay and tell them that if they weren't, I couldn't accept it. Then I'd laugh to show I was joking, but I never really was. I mean, in those days, I would have taken any free alcohol from anyone under any circumstances, but what I had meant was that I really, really hoped whoever was offering me the drink had done so because they wanted to ply me with booze and then hit on me. Two lesbians, drinking and flirting. I worked narratives of my newfound sexual identity into countless papers for class, probably to the droll amusement of the more liberal faculty and to the annoyance of others. Looking back, I could see that I was desperate for people to see this thing about me that I'd only just discovered and that I found so amazing. I wanted to make friends who were on the same journey of self-discovery, and, truthfully, I was always hoping that some woman would hear me declare my sexuality and decide she wanted to pursue me.

Almost no one ever had.

And here I was, in the truck of a veritable stranger who knew I was attracted to her. And now I knew that she knew, and she knew that I knew that she knew. Since I wasn't nineteen and shiny—nope, I was thirty-two and in theory a lot more mature about such things—I didn't feel exhilarated. I felt like a major dork. It was going to be a very long drive.

"I'm fine," I lied, staring at the empty pavement ahead. I wanted to change the subject, but I couldn't think of anything else to talk about it. I heard myself ask, "So, um, how could you tell, because I'm pretty straight-passing?"

Great opening salvo for a normal conversation, Dana. What sparkling repartee.

To her credit, Charlie didn't mock. "I don't know. I guess there's something about your energy."

When I was in college, the world had been a lot simpler. There were straight people, gay people, bi people, and trans people. Four categories, that was it. I was among the second category, and we identified each other with "gaydar," which basically meant we drew on admittedly awful stereotypes about hair, fashion, and speech to make presumptions about who was gay without asking them directly. That was pretty much what I'd done with Charlie. These days, such assumptions weren't really as socially acceptable. People came in all kinds of genders and sexualities, and my assumption that Charlie was a lesbian because of her deep voice and androgynous hair and clothes was anachronistic at best, offensive at worst.

"And you...you're...?" I waited a moment to see how she'd complete the sentence. Which identity labels did she affix to herself? When she didn't immediately answer, I backpedaled. "Is that too forward a question?"

"No, I guess not, since we've talked about you." She tossed me a quick look, I suspected to gauge my willingness to accept whatever she might be about to say. "I'm queer, too. I don't like the word 'lesbian.' I guess I just don't always feel like a girl."

"Do you identify as trans?"

Charlie reflected on this for a moment. "No. Maybe? I think genderqueer is more suitable."

I didn't say anything while I absorbed this information. Had I incorrectly read Charlie's interest in me then? Had I misidentified her when I thought she was a "her" in the first place? When she'd first stuck her head out of the truck window, I hadn't been certain of her gender. What was it that had made me so quickly assume Charlie and I were the same?

"What pronouns do you prefer?" I hoped my voice conveyed my sincere interest in the answer. At work we all included our pronouns on the bottom of our email signatures. Mine read: "Dana Gottfried, Assistant Executive Development Officer, she/her/hers." It was a move the diversity committee had recommended, and we'd all adopted it pretty eagerly. Since Charlie hadn't offered pronouns of her own, I was genuinely curious, and I didn't want her to think I was about to pronounce judgment on her.

"They. 'She' is okay. My family all call me 'she.'" She gave another look my way, and I sensed that some of her swagger had been deflated by this very personal discussion. I wanted to reassure her that this changed nothing about our time together.

"That's pretty cool."

Oh, wow, that was probably the worst possible thing that could have slid out of my mouth. What a loser I was. Not only did I lack panache, but I was borderline offensive. Cool?

Which part was cool exactly? That she was bucking the binary gender system or the part where her family didn't give a crap and still used pronouns Charlie didn't like? What was cool about that? I sounded like a loser with zero experience in this realm.

But if Charlie was genderqueer, what did that mean in terms of her sexuality? What types of people was she attracted to?

"Listen, Charlie, just now when you said I wouldn't be sitting here if you didn't know I was into women..."

"I'm sorry about that," she said softly. "If I made you uncomfortable."

"Uncomfortable" was one way to put it. Downright squirmy was another. But had I read the moment wrong? If Charlie wasn't a lesbian, was she still into lesbians? Was someone as straight-passing and bland as me even a blip on her radar? Maybe she had pulled over to help me because she thought it was the right thing to do, not because of my desperate need to believe someone found me attractive.

I summoned the courage to be frank. "That's not what I meant. I just meant—you were expressing interest in me, right?"

"You got a girlfriend somewhere and need me to back off?"

"Need me to back off" meant she was on. I hadn't imagined the flirting. I tried not to react like a schoolgirl with a crush as I admitted, "I most definitely do not have a girlfriend somewhere or anywhere."

"All right then." The arrogant quality of her voice had returned. She looked at me once more, this time letting her gaze linger as she arched an eyebrow. "Then just sit back and enjoy the ride."

I blushed even harder that time and wondered if there would be anything left of me besides ruptured blood vessels and a puddle by the time we got to Chicago.

We drove in comfortable silence, letting the audiobook narrator fill the void. I began to pay attention to the story, finding it wasn't that difficult to guess what I had missed and follow along. A different voice alerted us that we had reached the end of the first CD when Charlie pulled off the two-lane highway we'd been taking. We made a left turn onto a one-lane road that cut through some fields, which I imagined would be seven feet high with corn in the summer but now were brown and dotted white with the remaining snow. After a few minutes, the pavement gave way to gravel, and the truck rumbled along, bouncing us off the bench seat every time we hit a rock, until we made another left turn onto a dirt path and into a copse of trees.

At this point, the murder mystery in the background initiated a series of thoughts in my overactive brain. Charlie had taken me down roads I didn't know the name of. She'd told me she lived in Goshen, but I hardly knew where that was, and there was certainly no town nearby that I'd seen. As the truck inched into the woods, the smarter part of my brain began sending red alerts to my pulse. Danger could easily lie ahead. The fact that Charlie had been agreeable and flirtatious did not preclude the possibility that she was a serial killer. Maybe stalking the highway for victims was her M.O. And now I was stranded here with her, making one stupid choice today after another, all of which had led me to my death.

Or to an A-frame house bordering a small lake in a clearing. It looked quaint and expensive and like it would be the top-rated property on a rental website. There was a flat lawn that led down to the lake, and a wooden deck off the side of the house had stairs down to a dock. Families would come for long summer weeks, their kids jumping off the dock into the lake all day while the dads grilled burgers for dinner. Couples would rent the place for romantic winter getaway weekends. There was probably a fireplace inside, and people would take turns reading pages of books and rubbing each other's feet.

What I didn't see at the cute A-frame house was any sign that a rusty truck pig farmer lived there. The clearing was big by city standards, but it was hardly an expanse for growing crops and raising livestock. There was no barn for horses.

Charlie must have sensed my concern and confusion. "It's my house," she explained. "It's safe. If you don't trust me, you don't have to come in."

"You live here?"

"Yup."

"Do you own it?" Again I regretted how crass I sounded. The question stemmed from my expectation that Charlie would live in a ramshackle shanty with pigs trotting in and out, maybe something like that old television show *Green Acres*. Now that we were parked in front of "Charming Lakeside Cabin, sleeps four, $89 a night," I wondered how someone in a beat-up truck could afford such a nice house.

"I've rented it for a few years now." She followed my sight line to the house. "Something wrong?"

A lot of things were wrong with it, but mostly I noticed the yard was empty. "Where are the pigs?"

Charlie was clearly trying hard not to laugh at me. I thought it was a legitimate question, given her profession. "They don't live at my house, Dana." Her tone indicated I had been so foolish that it didn't even warrant clarification about where the pigs *did* live. She pushed open the driver's side door. "Just give me a few minutes, and I'll get my things packed. I started last night, so it shouldn't take too long."

I didn't answer and didn't get out of the truck, though I wanted to. I wanted to see the inside of the house, to figure out if my perception of Charlie had been completely off or if there were dead bodies in the basement or what. None of this was adding up.

By the time I decided I really did want to see inside and I wasn't going to be murdered with an ax, Charlie had already gone in. I figured it would be rude to let myself in, and I didn't want to seem like the kind of person who had trouble making decisions, so I was stuck in the truck. Charlie had left the key in the ignition, so the heat was still running. That was probably a good sign she didn't intend to murder me. I could have driven off with the truck and escaped my impending murder if I'd wanted to.

I didn't keep track of how long she took to get her things. Longer than a few minutes, but then again, I didn't have the audiobook to keep my interest in her absence. While she was gone, I couldn't help wondering how the interior of the house looked. Was this the kind of place that looked promising on the outside, only to be a complete mess of dirty dishes and furniture with the stuffing coming out and vinyl floor tiles inside? Or was this the classic open-concept, granite countertop American dream home? I doubted it. For one thing, the cabin was spacious but not a mansion. It looked older than the new millennium trend, and those houses were usually built in clusters in developments with street names like Cathy Court and Elizabeth Lane. On closer inspection, I could see that the cabin had some chipped and peeling paint. One of the downstairs windows was cracked, and I didn't even see a garage. No wonder the truck was rusting. This was more in line with what I had been envisioning.

Eventually, she came out the front door with an army green canvas duffel, which she slung into the truck's flatbed next to my suitcase. There was a lot of rustling around, and I craned backward to look out the rear window. She was stretching a tarp across the flatbed to protect our luggage.

I rolled my window down and leaned out. "Do you need help with that?"

Charlie pulled a length of rope taut in one fluid motion, then deftly tied it into a knot. "You just sit there and look pretty, darlin'."

I was kind of pissed off by what she said. I was also kind of delighted.

She finished tying the tarp down, and then she went back into the house.

I waited another ten minutes or so, wondering what she could be doing if she'd already brought out her bags. Feeding a cat? Going to the bathroom?

She emerged once more, this time with two plastic travel mugs bearing the name of a chain of gas stations. She tucked one in the crook of her elbow and wrenched the driver's side door open. She artfully swung inside without spilling any of the contents of the mugs. She handed me one.

"I made some coffee. Is it too late in the afternoon for you to drink it?"

I accepted the mug gratefully. The diner coffee had been too weak, more like hot water that soothes a cold throat than a spike of caffeine to perk up a tired traveler, and nothing that satisfied a true coffee addict's need. I took a tentative sip of

Charlie's coffee, careful not to burn my tongue, and hoped it would be stronger.

It was espresso. With frothy soy milk. Soy milk has a definitive vanilla and earthy taste that is different from the taste of cow's milk, which is more watery and sour. I knew it was soy milk the moment it hit my palate. Charlie had made me a soy latte.

Unsure what this gesture said about Charlie or her feelings toward me, I could nevertheless feel a smile creeping up my face. I greedily drank my treat as Charlie, ever the enigmatic road companion, swung the truck around the yard and led us back to the main road. Soon we were headed to the interstate and the Indiana-Illinois state line.

CHAPTER FIVE

Charlie made for an amiable traveling companion, aware of when to push me and when to leave me alone. We chatted about trivial things, such as the discovery that we both secretly liked to use the Taco Bell drive-through. We also talked about more serious subjects, such as shared concern over global politics and domestic civil rights. We didn't talk anymore about our gender and sexual identities, though I did hear myself mentioning Mitchell Wormerstein once in the context of a conversation about whether cats were superior to dogs. It reminded me of the time Mitchell had given me a puffy cat sticker for Valentine's Day. Stickers of any sort had been a premium commodity in grade school, and puffy stickers were extra special. Mitchell had sworn it was a gesture of friendship, but now that he was down the street from Nana, I had to wonder if the sticker gift had been motivated by a crush on me.

Charlie listened to this story, and many others, while sharing some of her own. I noticed she didn't talk about her family or any romantic interests, but she had a lot to say about the books she'd read and the philosophies she was contemplating. Charlie told me about *kintsugi*, the Japanese process of repairing broken pottery with gold thread to show the beauty in the cracks. She was deeply contemplative, not at all the thoughtless manual laborer I'd expected her to be, and the idea of embracing and celebrating imperfection clearly resonated with her on some deep spiritual level. I vowed to look up the concept once I was home.

Since Charlie hadn't planned on making a long road trip that day, she hadn't filled her gas tank. We had to stop for gas in Portage at one of those giant gas stations that had fifteen pumps for cars and an entire separate wing for truck parking. By that point, I was desperate to pee from the slushy and multiple cups of coffee I'd had, but I didn't think Charlie should have to pay for the gas.

"Here," I said, thrusting my credit card at her. "I insist."

"I don't need your money, Dana."

"I don't think you do," I agreed. "I'm offering to pay for the gas because you're driving me."

"I'd be going this way anyway." Charlie leapt out of the truck and slammed the door shut. I wasn't sure how being nice and offering to pay for a tank of gas had offended her, but if she wanted to freeze her butt off while she pumped, fine. I was going inside, where it was warm and where I could enjoy a nice long visit to the bathroom.

Inside the station was so brightly lit it resembled an airport at night. The overhead music was Bruce Springsteen's "Santa Claus Is Comin' to Town." I shielded my eyes with a hand and wished I could cover my ears as I made my way past the racks of audiobooks Charlie so loved, display cases of replacement cell phone batteries and chargers, and finally a rack of camouflage sweatshirts with catchy phrases like "Don't tread on me" and "Give me liberty or give me death" and images of guns. I hustled to the bathroom.

I found an empty stall that didn't look totally disgusting and finally achieved sweet release on my bladder. While I was going, I heard the door creak open and someone come in. From the gap under the stall door, I could see Charlie's boots. She went into the stall beside me, and the door swung shut, shaking mine as well. I could hear Charlie pee, and I knew Charlie could hear me pee, and I hated having that kind of bodily intimacy with someone I'd just met. I resented the stall divider for giving the pretense that we had any kind of privacy.

I was also a little surprised that Charlie had strolled into the women's bathroom so confidently. I wasn't sure where I expected her to go, but nonetheless the sight of her boots under the stall divider wasn't what I had anticipated. When I finished, I flushed the toilet, stepped out, and washed my hands.

Charlie came out as I was drying my hands. I held my breath to see what she would do. When she turned the faucet on and soaped up, I breathed a sigh of relief. No way could I ride in the truck with someone who didn't wash.

From the sink next to mine, she caught my eyes in the mirror. "You're a long pee-er."

"Excuse me?"

"You pee for a long time. Do you always do that?"

I was flabbergasted. What kind of person timed someone else's pee longevity? And then actually talked about it? I looked around the bathroom to see if anyone else might hear. We were thankfully alone.

"That embarrass you?"

"Yes!" I hissed. "You can't—you can't just come in here and measure people's pee and then tease them about it! I happen to have been holding it for a very long time!"

Charlie dried her hands in one quick back and forth motion on a flimsy paper towel, then chucked it into the hole in the counter for the trash. I bet her hands were still wet. I hated that feeling. "If you say so."

I trailed out behind her, fuming and humiliated. Did I take too long to go the bathroom? I had no idea. Unlike Charlie, I'd never timed myself.

We didn't get very far past the camouflage patriot gear before Charlie halted in her tracks, and I crashed into her back comically.

Except the situation wasn't funny.

A man tall enough for me to see over Charlie's head was facing her menacingly. He had on the same construction boots and jeans as her and a neon orange ski cap on his head. His face was ruddy with cold and covered in stubble. He looked maybe forty, forty-five.

"Is there a problem, sir?" I was naive enough not to have felt any qualms at that point. Charlie obviously did, or she wouldn't have stopped cold like that. Foolish me, I didn't know what she was worried about.

"My wife told me she couldn't go in the bathroom because she saw this guy in there." He was referring to Charlie. From a few feet away, I saw a similarly aged woman and a teenage daughter scurry toward the restrooms. They must have been waiting for Charlie to exit.

"I'm sorry for any inconvenience," Charlie mumbled.

I fumed again for a different reason. Seeing the wind knocked out of Charlie's sails made me want to punch this guy in the face. "There were plenty of open stalls," I told him. "Your wife could have easily come in."

"I'm not going to let her put herself in harm's way."

First of all, she would hardly have been in the way of any harm except for the mental damage that having someone time her pee length could have caused. Also, let her? He wouldn't let her? Could she only go to the bathroom when he deemed it safe enough? I hated this guy.

"You're towering over us. Do we really look that harmful?"

"Cut it out, Dana," Charlie warned me.

I grabbed Charlie's sleeve and pushed past her to face the man. "What is your problem? My friend has on a man's coat, so you assume she's a pervert? Your wife has never worn your coat? Or maybe it's the haircut? Didn't you live through the seventies? You didn't have long hair back then? Get over yourself. We're trying to get somewhere, same as you. Only we're not assholes enough to insert ourselves into other people's business."

I tried to shove past him, but he was a wall of solid meat, and he stood his ground. I could either back down or try to save face. Not willing to let him win, I tried to slide between him and a rack of chips, and all the cellphone wrappers crumpled noisily as I did. I could hear a few bags plop to the ground. I couldn't go back and pick them up, though. This was a mission. I held my head high as I walked toward the door.

Charlie was silent as she followed me outside, and it wasn't until we were back in the truck that she let loose. "What was that, Dana? I told you to cut it out!"

"What are you talking about? I was defending you! You're welcome."

"Did I ask you to defend me?"

"That guy was out of line."

"Do you think provoking him is going to get him back in line? That's how people end up killed, Dana. This isn't about political grandstanding. It's about survival."

I thought Charlie should show a lot more gratitude, frankly, and I snapped. "How are you supposed to survive if you don't stand up for yourself? And why did you use the women's room anyway? You couldn't have gone in the men's? Do you know how uncomfortable that made me?"

"Oh, you too, huh? You're just like that guy!"

"No, I am not! I wasn't uncomfortable because you're the wrong gender! I was uncomfortable because I don't like people hearing me pee!"

"Well, excuse me, next time I'll go in the men's room, where I'll have to use a stall and be even more of an outcast because Delicate Dana doesn't want me to hear her urinate! Or maybe you'd prefer if I just go in the alley like an animal!"

I crossed my arms over my chest angrily. "Screw you," I said quietly. "That is *not* what I meant, and you know it."

Charlie's voice softened in tone. "You need to quit trying to rescue me. The gas payment, the bathroom. Just let me be, Dana. It's important to me."

"*Okay.*" I said it the way a little kid would tell their parents they understood something they didn't understand at all because they didn't want to get yelled at anymore.

"Dana." She reached across the truck and touched my elbow. I let my arms come uncrossed. "This is all part of what it means to be me. I'm sorry you had to see it, but that was pretty much nothing. It gets a lot worse."

"I can't imagine."

"No, you really can't."

"I just wanted to help."

"I know, but it's important to me to decide how and when to stand up for myself. Can you understand that?"

"Yeah, but that's not what the gas money was about."

"Okay." Charlie said it with as much conviction as I had.

"Can you start the engine? It's cold in here."

Charlie obliged, and we drove back to the highway. We didn't talk for at least another exit—and in Indiana, that can be a long time. We didn't put the audiobook back on either. The atmosphere in the truck was tense. I wasn't sure how things had managed to get so strained between us, and I wasn't sure how to fix it. I only knew that my position hadn't been fully explained, and that frustrated me. I didn't like not being able to say everything on my mind.

I could see Charlie's point about fighting her own battles. How could anyone expect to be treated fairly if they weren't even given the chance to speak for themselves? To have someone else always rushing to the rescue probably felt demoralizing, and Charlie was right. It wasn't my call whether she stood and fought or backed down. That was Charlie's call to make. I had had good intentions, but they were misguided. I wasn't supposed to be a savior. That only made Charlie someone who need saving.

At last I could bear the uncomfortable silence no more. "I'm sorry."

Charlie nodded, her eyes never straying from the road. "Thank you."

"I peed in an alley once." It was true, but it wasn't anything I had planned on sharing. Now it seemed like a peace offering. "It's not so bad."

It worked. Charlie smiled despite herself. "Why did you do that?"

I smiled, too, happy to have a follow-up question that meant the tension had evaporated. "I was in college, and my friends and I were at this bar, and I wasn't twenty-one yet. They didn't card me at first, but after I'd had a few drinks, I saw the bartender talking to the server who'd been taking care of our table, and they were looking in my direction. My friends and I started to panic because everyone else was already twenty-one, but I didn't even have a fake ID. At that point, I'd had a whole glass of ice water and two whiskey sours, and I really, really had to pee. Then the server started coming toward our table with the bartender, and we were convinced we were all going to be arrested—although in reality they probably would have just asked us to leave—but we didn't want to get arrested, so we ran out of the bar. Only we'd had a tab going, and they had someone's credit card, and we hadn't paid yet. So then the server was chasing us for another reason, so we wouldn't leave the credit card behind, and we were trying to figure out where to hide because we were so dumb we didn't realize that's why she was chasing us—okay, not dumb, just drunk—and I couldn't hold my pee anymore. We all ran to the alley behind the bar and hid behind the dumpster, and I just pulled my jeans down and let loose right there. I didn't even step away from the others." I shook my head, remembering the blurry night. "I'm pretty sure other people were in the splash zone."

"Did the server catch up to you?"

"Yeah." Why had I thought this was a good story to share? "She came down the alley to the dumpsters with the credit card, and she was more worried about us leaving it behind, only at that point, she saw me with my pants down, peeing all over where she had to take out the garbage at the end of the night."

"What did she do?"

"Not what *she* did," I said. "We didn't wait to see what she did. We took off running. Only my pants weren't up yet, and I fell flat on my face."

"So you're flat on your face in an alley, pants down, butt facing up for the world?"

"Yeah." My cheeks burned hot. "Eventually my friends came back for me, and they helped me pull my pants up. The server explained what was going on with the credit card, and she told us that if we didn't get in a cab and go home, she was going to call the police and post a picture of us behind the bar. I totally thought she meant she had a picture of me peeing or with my pants down, so I begged my friends to go home. Fast."

Charlie drummed her thumb on the steering wheel for a second, and I held my breath to see how she'd react. Massive oversharing on my part. Why didn't I decide to tell her about the time we talked our way into a private party at the top of the Hancock building and ended up drinking champagne with the governor of South Dakota? That was a way better underage drinking story!

"You're weird, Dana," Charlie finally pronounced.

Rude. Not wrong, but still rude. But at least she was talking to me again.

Since things had loosened up, I thought I'd ask Charlie for some of her own stories. "What about you? Any wacky and wild stories from your college years?"

"Plenty."

"That you're going to share with me?"

The thumb-drumming continued for another moment. "Okay, I'll bite."

"I'm all ears."

Charlie looked across the cab at me. "When I say I'm about to tell you a story, and you interrupt to say you're listening, you're actually not listening. You're talking."

I hadn't really thought of it that way before. Could I say I was sorry, or was that talking again? I opted to stick my tongue out at her.

"Do you want to hear the story or not?"

"Sorry," I mumbled.

Charlie kept her eyes on the road while she talked. "I went to college downstate, at Urbana-Champaign, but we Chicago kids found each other pretty quickly at orientation. At first, we were probably only friends because we were so weirded out by being in such a small place surrounded by rural areas. And maybe we were weirded out by the local kids. I hate saying that, but it's probably true. Anyway, it was about halfway through my first year that I started to realize we weren't only geographic misfits. We were all queer. We started coming out, one by one, and it was this bond that kept us together. A group of them starting doing theater together and loved it. I was always in a lab, since I was majoring in food science, so I didn't have as much time to goof around as the rest of them. But we had a standing weekly date to go to the nearby Denny's at midnight on Saturday to catch up with each other. Nobody ever missed. It didn't matter how much homework we had or whether we had girlfriends or boyfriends. We always made time for it."

It sounded like Charlie had found a new family among these friends. I'd had good friends in college, too, but mine were, like me, prone to flaking out on plans and sometimes emotionally unreliable. It would have been nice to have had that kind of loyalty, especially through the early days of coming out.

"They were theater kids," Charlie continued, "so someone was always up to something. They'd show up in costumes they stole from the wardrobe or in crazy makeup, and most of the time they'd act like nothing strange was going on. It was a game to see if they could spook the wait staff." She gave a small chuckle. "The best night was when my closest friend found a pair of crutches in the theater prop shop and used them all night for the hell of it. When the host saw him come hobbling in from the parking lot, she sat us at the nearest table and gave him an extra chair to prop up his leg. Several of the servers came to check on him. They made a real fuss. They gave him free dessert and everything. And after we paid our check, Clint stood up on both legs and yelled, 'It's a miracle!' We ran out of there as fast as we could, but we were laughing hysterically. I had no idea he was going to do that."

I liked hearing about Charlie's college shenanigans. But I noticed that the story was about someone else, and I wondered if she was always the serious one just along for the ride. Were all Charlie's favorite memories about things other people had done, or had Charlie created her own share of trouble? Did Charlie ever get to be the center of attention? Was that even something she craved?

"What?" she asked. "You're making a face."

"I am not!"

"You are. You're doing this." Charlie squinted her eyes and made duck lips.

I laughed with good nature. There was no way I was making that face, but she was perceptive. "I was thinking that story was really about someone else, and my story was about me. It made me wonder if you like to be in the spotlight."

"I do not. You?"

"Maybe? Not when it's because everyone's laughing at me. You really don't? You don't mind being in the wings like that? The supporting cast?"

"I'm hardly the supporting cast in my own life," Charlie pointed out. "I like observing the world. You learn a lot when you're not worrying about what you're doing and saying but watching what other people will do and say instead."

"That's a really thoughtful way to put it."

"Thanks." She winked at me. "We rushed out of that gas station so fast that I didn't have time to get something to drink. Are you thirsty?"

I dreaded stopping again. Every time we stopped, we added that much more time to the trip. But I was thirsty, too, and I had been hoping to get a package of Twizzlers at the gas station before our pit stop had been so rudely interrupted.

I knew I needed to get home to Highland Park. I wanted to. I felt the tether to that place slowly reeling me in. I was also beginning to scratch the surface of who Charlie was, and something indescribable in me wanted to slow the tether down long enough to keep scratching.

"It's okay if I stop for a drink?"

"Yes," I conceded. "Can we go through a drive-through?"

"You got it. I do not need another face-to-face encounter."

"Charlie? Thank you for explaining what the incident at the bathroom felt like from your perspective. I'm sorry you have to go through that. I hope you know I only had good intentions when I yelled at that guy. But I get what you mean about fighting your own battles. I guess I just want you to know that I'd be willing to fight alongside you."

"Thank you," Charlie said, guiding the truck down an off-ramp toward a McDonald's. "It's nice to have an ally to do that."

CHAPTER SIX

I llinois and Indiana were connected in the north by a massive bridge that allowed drivers willing to pay a high price to pass over the less economically privileged parts of both states in a shortcut to Chicago. It was a toll bridge with about a hundred different lanes for paying tolls, yet somehow I had never been able to avoid sitting in line for a good ten minutes. That day was worse, as so many other cars were, like us, trying to get somewhere to be with their families for the holiday. As we waited behind two minivans and a semitruck, another of the audiobook CDs concluded, and Charlie absentmindedly ejected it and replaced it with the next in the series.

"What time is it?" I wondered. The sky had grown dark somewhere before the state line, but while Charlie's radio had a CD player, it didn't have a digital face with a clock. I fumbled around for my purse and phone.

"It's five," Charlie reported. "Don't forget we gained an hour."

"I'm getting hungry, but we're so close now, I think Nana would kill me if I spoiled my dinner. How much longer do you think this toll booth is going to take?"

"I don't know, Dane." I liked that. Dane. Like we were old friends. "I'm guessing 94 is completely backed up because of the holiday. Check on your phone."

My phone was once again nearing the end of its battery lifespan, thanks to not fully charging it at the diner and stupidly forgetting to tell it to stop searching for a Wi-Fi signal for the last two hours. I fished the new cord I'd bought out of my purse and held it up for Charlie's approval. She nodded and pointed to a spot below the radio where a USB adapter was plugged into the cigarette lighter, and I inserted my cord.

My map app showed nothing but red dots along the highway all the way to Highland Park. Charlie was right. Five o'clock was rush hour in Chicago on a normal day. Tonight, everyone on the south side was trying to get north for Christmas Eve, causing extra congestion. Even though we were only about forty miles from Nana's house, the app estimated it would take us another two hours to get there. I groaned.

"What do you need, darlin'?" Charlie inched the truck forward in line. "Food? Bathroom? Want to call to check on your nana again?"

"I don't know," I heard myself whine. "I'm sick of sitting in traffic like this. I'd rather be moving."

"Okay, I got you covered."

When it was finally our turn to pay, Charlie handed over some crumpled dollar bills, waving off my offer to contribute, which was good because the only time I had cash on hand was when I knew I'd go through the tollway. And my toll money was still tucked neatly in the compartment between the two front seats of my car, along with a *Best of Wayne Newton* CD someone had once given me as a joke.

After paying the toll, we crossed the high bridge into Illinois. I hated that bridge. It gave me the creeps. I was always convinced my car was somehow going to flip over the concrete barrier and go crashing down on the roofs of the little bungalows below. My palms sweated, and I willed myself to breathe steadily and not scream at Charlie for driving one-handed.

As soon as we had crossed the bridge, Charlie put on her turn signal and changed into the right lane. She steered for the nearest exit.

"What are you doing?"

"You said you wanted to keep moving," she answered breezily as she led us onto surface streets. "This way, we won't be stuck in traffic."

Did she really plan to drive along streets with traffic lights for the next forty miles? How exactly would that be more efficient than the highway?

"Do me a favor," she said, "and pull up directions. I'm pretty sure I remember how to get to Lake Shore Drive from here, but just in case there's traffic or I forget. It's been a while since I came this way."

In horror at her absolutely flawed decision-making, I stabbed the map app on my phone again. We cruised through one intersection, then followed everyone else in a left turn that led us to a two-lane street lined with parked cars and bumper-to-bumper traffic. We rolled to a stop. I was never going to get home.

"I don't understand why you got off the highway!" I didn't know until that moment how shrill I could be. "Honestly, what were you thinking? This is going to take forever!"

"We're fine, Dane."

I did not appreciate her use of a casual nickname in a moment like this.

We inched our way to the intersection right as the light turned yellow, and Charlie hesitated instead of plowing through it, and then when she started to go forward, the light turned red. We were stuck in the middle of the intersection, blocking the traffic coming in the opposite direction. Cars on both sides of us began honking in fury.

"What are you doing! Why did you stop!"

"All right, I screwed up!" Charlie yelled back. "I can't just turn around and go back."

She meant go back out of the intersection, I knew, but I decided to interpret it as a larger critique on her navigational choices.

"That's exactly what you can do. Turn around in that parking lot after the light goes green and get back on the highway."

I covered my face with my hand for the remainder of the red light, so I wouldn't have to make eye contact with any of the angry drivers trying to squeeze past us. The light felt interminably long, but finally it turned green and the cars in front of us crept forward enough that we could slink out of the intersection with our proverbial tail between our legs.

We rolled slowly toward the parking lot. A row of cars moving at an equal crawl on the other side of the street blocked our chances of being able to make a left, so Charlie didn't even make an attempt to turn around. She could have put her signal on, but I knew from experience we'd be waiting an hour for someone coming the opposite direction to take pity on us and let us make the turn. I hated Chicago traffic at that moment. I hated Charlie more.

"This was the worst idea ever!"

"Calm down," Charlie snapped. She reached blindly for my phone on the bench seat between us and held it in my direction. "Why don't you do something useful, like look up the traffic, so we can see if there's a better route?"

"The better route is the one above our heads."

"We were stuck there."

"The congestion would have cleared up."

"It'll clear up down here, too."

"Are you always this combative?" I wondered. "Can you ever just admit you made a mistake and—"

Screeeeeech. Slam. Honnnnnnnnnnnk.

I watched in horror as the second and third cars in front of us slammed together. The blue Prius immediately before us swerved sharply left to avoid being the third car in the accident, and an oncoming car drove up on the sidewalk to avoid hitting the Prius. From our view in the truck above the smaller cars, I saw the whole thing in a flash of seconds. I clenched my fists and pushed my feet against the floorboards, as if that would will the truck to stop. But Charlie skillfully hit the brakes, preventing a pile-up.

My blood ran cold, and my breathing accelerated. I thought of my mom and dad driving home from a night out and when—*Crash!*—suddenly everything had stopped for them. And for me.

"Oh shit," Charlie murmured. She eased the truck as far to the side of the road as she could. We couldn't pull all the way over because there were cars parked against the curb. Charlie put the truck in park and leapt out.

"Where are you going?" I shouted, but she was already gone. Crippled with the fear that someone else had died, I stayed. I braced my sweaty palms on the dashboard and tried to breathe. The *ba-boom ba-boom* of my heart was loud enough to hear in the truck. My eyes were leaking tears, but even if they hadn't been, I couldn't see. The world around me had turned into a blur of confusion and terror. We had not been hurt, I reminded myself. The person in the Prius had not been hurt. No one had been on the sidewalk when the other car jumped the curb. I didn't know if the people in the other two cars had been hurt.

The car behind us honked viciously, jolting me to action. The only way I could see if someone was hurt was to get out of the truck. If they were hurt and I didn't get out, and they died, I would die right there, that night, never making it back to Nana, and she'd lose almost everyone she loved to car accidents.

I leaned toward the passenger door handle, but Charlie had pulled too close to the parked cars. I couldn't open my door. I slid instead across the bench seat and jumped out the driver's side. I surveyed the accident scene.

Charlie spotted me and trotted over. "Dane? Dana? Hey, are you with me?"

"My parents."

"Dana, stay with me, okay? I might need your help." Charlie put herself directly in my line of vision. "Allies in the battlefield, right?"

I nodded. Charlie wiped my cheeks with her gloved fingers. She cupped my face. I thought she might kiss my forehead, and I wanted her to. My mom used to do that when I was scared.

"I'm gonna go check on the car, okay?"

I nodded again and followed in a daze.

Two cars ahead of us, a black SUV was crumpled into the trunk of a silver sedan. The driver of the sedan, a young man, was still behind the wheel, an exploded air bag covering him. His chest didn't look crushed, but he was clearly dazed and a little singed.

"Call—" Charlie started, but I had already grabbed her phone out of her hand and dialed 911. The sight of him still alive brought me back to life. He needed me. I could save him. But I had to act fast.

I gave the emergency operator our location to the best of my knowledge while Charlie talked to the driver. She got him out of the car and onto the pavement, and then she encouraged him to stay put until the paramedics arrived in case he had injuries he didn't realize. The driver of the SUV got out, looking frazzled but unmarked.

"I'm sorry, oh my God, I'm so sorry," she repeated until Charlie yelled at her to quiet down and stand to the side. At least the woman didn't attempt to take off. Not that she could in the traffic. The northbound lane was now completely stuck, and the southbound land was creeping by one car at a time as they had to maneuver around the blue Prius. The Prius driver didn't bother getting out to see if everyone was okay. He was on the phone, acting as if we'd all greatly inconvenienced him with this delay. His shittiness enraged me in light of the severity of what was going on.

It was Christmas Eve, and none of us were going to get where we wanted to go any time soon. One person might not even be going home tonight at all if the paramedics decided the Corolla driver needed to go to the hospital. As much as I wished we hadn't come this way and seen this accident, only a complete jerk would view the situation as an inconvenience.

Charlie was still talking to the injured driver, and the lady who'd caused the accident was still blubbering to me.

"I really don't know how that happened. I was paying attention, and then I looked down for one second, and that car came out of nowhere."

I didn't believe her at all. How could a car come out of nowhere in bumper to bumper traffic? "You could have killed people!" I lashed out. "Someone could have fucking died!"

"Hey, hey, hey, Dana!" Charlie called from a yard away. "Not helping!"

"I'm sorry," the woman blubbered. "I'm so sorry."

Granted, I had seen the crash but not what caused it because I had been too busy shouting at Charlie—shouting, I realized, with enough distraction to have made Charlie get into an accident, too. We were damn lucky she was so calm under pressure.

The woman ran a hand through her blown-out blond hair, but when she put it down, a patch of her hair was matted and red.

"Lady, you're bleeding!"

"What?" She looked at her hand and nearly fainted. I caught her by the armpits and helped her to the side of the road, where she collapsed onto the curb. She said she didn't mind if I looked at her head, which I did as tenderly as possible. There was a cut along her scalp and possibly some glass shards embedded around it. I took her hand by the wrist and turned her palm upward. There was more glass stuck in her hand. Her windshield was intact, so I wasn't sure what it was, but she definitely needed medical attention, too.

"Was there something made of glass in your car?"

"My angel?" For a moment I thought she was delirious, but she explained, "I have a crystal angel hanging from my windshield for good luck."

Some good luck. It had shattered into her head. Part of me felt she deserved it.

"Charlie!" I called. Charlie trotted over and examined our other patient.

"Do you feel like you hit your head?" she asked the woman patiently.

"I don't know—maybe? It all happened so fast."

"Your head wound doesn't look too bad. It's bleeding a lot, but the cut's not that deep. You should stay sitting. There's an ambulance on its way. We should have the EMTs check you out before you start walking around."

The woman grew visibly afraid. It was funny how she didn't seem to worry about how hurt the driver she hit was, but when faced with her own mortality, suddenly she was all quivering lips.

"Do you think I need stitches?"

"Probably," I snapped.

"I'm so sorry."

That refrain was getting old and wasn't getting us anywhere. The person who killed my parents had been sorry. He'd been drinking and hadn't realized his car was veering into the other lane. My dad had tried to swerve to avoid him. The drunk driver had plowed my parents' car into the ditch on their side of the road, where it had flipped onto its side. The other car hadn't even braked until it was halfway through the front of my dad's car. There hadn't been any hope for my mom's survival. My dad had died a day later.

"Have you been drinking?" I asked the driver now.

"No! I swear!" She didn't seem drunk, more like delirious from the accident. "Are you okay? You look really upset."

Her asking me that question shook me. I sank down onto the curb beside her. "I'm okay," I sobbed, sounding totally not okay. She cried back, and we hugged each other for a moment, taking comfort in the fact that we were both alive and relatively unharmed.

"I'm Dana," I managed to say at last.

"Elizabeth."

"Elizabeth, where were you headed tonight?" She didn't look as if she belonged in this part of town. She looked like someone who lived in a loft in the South Loop and who needed a sixteen-dollar raspberry mojito pronto.

"I—I was driving back from Gary," she said. "I work at a children's home."

Well, didn't I feel awful for misjudging her as a self-absorbed rich lady who rear-ended people because of her narcissism?

Channeling Charlie, I assured her, "We're going to make sure you're okay, and we're going to get you on your way home."

"I think my car is totaled."

I looked at her SUV. Now that I was an expert in totaled cars, I judged it wasn't actually so bad, probably because of its sheer size and power compared to the silver Corolla she'd hit. "Did your air bag go off?"

"I don't know. I think so. I jumped out pretty quickly."

Elizabeth was more injured and shaken than I'd realized. I squeezed her good hand compassionately. "I lost my car today. A stranger helped me."

"Like you're helping me now."

Soon enough the paramedics came, and Elizabeth and the other driver were examined. Both were taken to the hospital. Elizabeth needed stitches, and Charlie told the paramedics that the other driver had been fading in and out of lucidity. The police were only a moment behind them, followed by three different tow trucks hoping to score a paycheck from the wreckage. The blue Prius drove away as soon as a police officer took charge of the traffic, directing one lane and then the other to move past the accident. Charlie and I didn't leave, though. By that point, we felt too involved and were waiting for the police to tell us our duties were over before we felt comfortable leaving the scene.

While we waited, Charlie said, "You were great back there. You really pulled through."

"I was nothing compared to you."

"My car didn't die today. That must have made it hard for you."

"It's not that," I explained. "It was my parents."

"Your parents?"

"They died in a car accident."

"Shit, Dana, I didn't realize. Are you okay?"

"I think so. I think it was just really important to me that no one died tonight."

"Everyone's okay," Charlie assured me. "Thanks to you, everyone got the help they needed, and they're going to be fine. We're fine."

It was hardly thanks to me, but I welcomed Charlie's comfort.

One of the police officers interrupted us to ask for our side of the story. After repeating our contact information for him, in case the police needed to contact us with questions about what we'd seen, Charlie and I were finally told we could go.

We turned to walk back to the truck.

It was at an upright angle, suspended there by a giant chain connected to a tow truck.

"Noooooo!" Charlie called, running toward it.

The driver ignored her and continued hoisting Charlie's truck by the stupid chain attached to the underside of the engine.

"Why are you towing us?" I screamed, banging on the side of his truck.

He rolled the window down. "This your truck?" We nodded. "You've been blocking the street. That's a violation. Gotta tow you."

"What?! We were giving statements to the police!" Charlie explained.

"Need to park and meter for that."

"Are you kidding me? I was being a good citizen."

"There aren't any parking spaces!" I added. "The cars in front of us had an accident. Where were we supposed to go?"

The tow truck driver shrugged and rolled his window up. Charlie looked at me, eyes wide in panic. It was the first time I'd seen her lose her cool.

Think, Dana, I told myself. Hurry and think.

"The officer," I suggested. "We can ask him to call off the tow."

Together, we turned around. And together, we saw the squad car slowly drive off toward the next emergency.

"Damn it!" Charlie yelled.

We watched as our only means of transportation was driven away by the tow truck, and I felt a rising sense of despair that I would never make it to see Nana. We were so close now, and here I was, trapped south of the city by Charlie's stupidity and generosity. I wanted to cry.

CHAPTER SEVEN

O kay," Charlie said calmly. "Come on, Dane, it's not that bad. We can get a cab to the train station."

"There aren't any cabs in this neighborhood," I pointed out through my tears. They fell partly out of frustration, but they were also the result of all the intense emotions about my parents and witnessing an accident finally reaching their boiling point and spilling out my eyeballs. "We'll have to call for one, and how long will that take? We don't even know when the train schedule is."

"How's your phone battery?"

I handed Charlie her phone, which I'd used to call 911, and looked down. I wasn't wearing my coat because it had been too hot in the truck, and I hadn't realized it because I had been running on adrenaline. Now I was freezing cold. And my jean pockets were glaringly empty. I didn't have my purse on me. I whimpered.

"My wallet and phone just got towed."

Charlie shut her eyes. I braced for her wrath, but she didn't yell at me. I was glad. I didn't want her to be angry. I would get angry enough at myself in a few minutes, after the sense of hopelessness wore off. I'd probably get angry at her, too, and blame the whole situation on her, whether that was fair or not. Eventually I would go into active mode and figure out a plan. Right now, though, I just wanted to cry, and I wanted someone else to fix everything because mustering the energy to figure things out was beyond me.

On cue, Charlie began tapping her phone screen. "I'm calling a friend."

After thirty minutes of huddling together on the sidewalk, trying to stay warm, a silver BMW pulled alongside the parked cars, blocking traffic. As the other cars began honking, I flinched, expecting another accident, but Charlie yelled, "Come on!" She nearly shoved me into the back seat, and the car screeched off before Charlie had even fully shut the back door.

"It's been a long time, stranger." The driver made eye contact with Charlie through the rearview mirror. Her bag was on the front seat, so Charlie and I were sharing the back. I caught Charlie twisting her hands and wondered why she was so apprehensive. "Where am I taking you?"

"The city impound lot," I answered. "Do you know where that is?"

"It's under Wacker," Charlie replied. "I was towed another time. We should check on their hours, though."

"Don't they tow twenty-four seven?"

"Yeah, but they might not have a cashier to let people get their cars out twenty-four seven."

Well, that was obnoxious. How many people got towed at two in the morning and had to wander around aimlessly until the lot opened for business? They probably went to bars.

I could have used a drink. Except I had no money. And there was free wine at Nana's, if I could ever get there.

"I don't have a phone," I reminded Charlie.

Charlie lifted a hip off the seat to get her phone out of her back pocket. I tried not to stare at the fluid movements of her body, given the predicament we were in, but I couldn't help noticing. Everything about the way she moved turned me on.

"So...who are you?" The driver's crisp eyes found mine in the mirror. I thought she had seen me watching Charlie. She was as intimidating as the dark crimson lipstick that perfectly lined her lips. In the dim streetlights, I could see she had ivory skin and exquisite black winged eyeliner and long, dark lashes, but those feminine features didn't detract from her bite.

I pretended not to hear the hostility in her voice. "My name is Dana."

"Hello, Dana, I'm Caroline." She had a tinge of a British accent to her voice, more like an expatriate who'd spent too many years abroad than an actual Brit. She pronounced her words with precision. In the Chicago area, we tended to talk fast, slurring words together in a rush of breathlessness. I hadn't known this about our speech until I moved to Ohio, where people thought I sounded quaintly northern and was addicted to speed. Caroline didn't sound like that. She was perfectly composed but phony. I bet everything she did was deliberate. She was the kind of woman I wanted to be but could never manage to pull off.

"And how do you know our Charlie?" she asked.

I shot a glance at Charlie, wondering if she had even said she had a passenger when she had called for help and, if she had, how she had explained that we knew each other. "I'm just—"

"I got some information," Charlie interrupted. "The tow lot closes at six."

"It's already seven," Caroline informed us.

"So what does that mean?" I asked stupidly.

"You can't get your car back until tomorrow."

"Tomorrow's Christmas," Charlie said. "It'll have to be the day after at the earliest."

"My purse is in there! And my phone! Damn it!" I banged my fist on the window ledge. This stupid drive that I hadn't wanted to make in the first place was turning into an epic adventure that wouldn't die. It was frustrating to have come this far from Cleveland and to be so close to Nana's but stuck again. I had promised Nana I'd be there for dinner. I heard myself sniff. I hated the thought of letting Nana down on Christmas Eve, even if I didn't believe in the holiday. It wasn't about Christmas so much as it was about time to spend showing Nana how much she mattered to me.

"Hey," Charlie murmured too quietly for Caroline to hear, "it's okay. Do you want to borrow my phone?"

"Actually, yeah. Thank you."

I dialed Nana's home phone number, one of the few I knew by heart, but she didn't answer. That was a little concerning, since she usually stuck close to the phone when I was on the road. Sometimes she couldn't hear it ring if she was in a different room, or she'd fall asleep while watching TV and the ringing wouldn't wake her. I tried her cell phone next, but Nana wasn't the best at keeping it on her. She usually only paid attention to it when she was out of the house. There was no answer on her cell phone either.

Sometimes I worried that I'd call and get no answer, like tonight, not because Nana was asleep or in a different room but because something had happened to her. I had recently suggested we install cameras in a few spots of the house for moments like this, so I could see what was going on. Nana had vetoed that idea before I had even finished explaining how it would work. Understandably. I wouldn't want my granddaughter spying on me either, but since I lived so far, I wanted some reassurance as to what she was doing all day. If I called a couple of times and still couldn't get through, I would sometimes call Ruthie to double-check that everything was fine. Ruthie was more robust and didn't seem to mind making the trek over to Nana's to check on her.

If it was already seven, maybe Nana was at Ruthie's right that moment. Hopefully she was in the company of her friends. Maybe she was drinking alcohol that conflicted with her medication and that she was forbidden to drink but did anyway. I'd given up that fight. She was eighty-five. If she wanted to drink wine, so be it. And maybe she was eating party food. Nana never had much of an appetite, but she took comfort when gatherings had tables laden with food. She had told me it was because she was born during the Depression and had grown up under rationing for World War II, but I was born in the prosperity of the 1980s and felt the same way.

With any luck, Nana was at that moment so busy conversing with Franklin Silverman, the neighborhood octogenarian bachelor, that she wouldn't mind my tardiness. I could have called Ruthie's house to verify, but, stupidly, I had never memorized her number.

I remembered that I had assured Mitchell Wormerstein that I'd be home for dinner and that his invitation to Nana was not necessary. The vision of Nana and Franklin clinking wine glasses and chortling with laughter dissolved before my eyes. Instead, I pictured Nana on the sofa, nodding off but trying not to. There was probably a pot of coffee scalding in the kitchen. She had probably made it to keep herself awake and to share when I got home and we sat at the kitchen table, catching up with each other.

I glumly handed the phone back to Charlie.

She and Caroline were talking, and although I hadn't been listening while I tried to reach Nana, I could tell there was something strained in their interactions. Charlie ignored me as she took her phone back and did the same hip thrust to put it back into her pocket.

"...really can't believe you," Caroline was saying.

"You had a choice," Charlie replied.

"No, I didn't."

They both let the charged words hang in the air.

"Well, if the tow lot is closed," Caroline said finally, "what is your backup plan?"

Charlie finally looked at me as if to ask what I wanted to do. That put me in an awkward position, since I wanted to get to Highland Park, but I didn't have any money to help me get there.

"I'd like to take the Metra," I said quietly, "but my purse..."

"I got you, darlin'." Then more loudly, "How about the Metra station, Care? Do you know how to get there from here?"

"Care" looked extremely put out by this request. I wasn't particularly keen on this nickname, especially as it made my "Dane" seem less special and more like a standard formula Charlie used to shorten the names of people she needed to speak to. "Care" pursed her crimson lips. It occurred to me I did not know where she had come from and where she had planned on going. Were we making her drive all over the city in the wrong direction?

"You'd better look up the train schedule," she said.

"There's always a train at thirty-five minutes after the hour," I replied confidently. "The last one is at ten thirty-five." I had learned that in college when I'd take the train downtown to meet friends, go to fancy restaurants, or see concerts. Inevitably, I'd lose track of the time and find myself speeding in a cab to the station and running to jump on the last train to Highland Park before it left the platform. Because one thing I had not been in college was organized.

"Not lately," Caroline said. "They've eliminated trains due to budget cuts. Plus, they're on holiday service. It's been all over the news." She shook her head at how pathetically out of touch I was.

I resisted the urge to roll my eyes. Since I had moved away, I had learned that Chicagoans liked to lord their urbane knowledge over non-city folks. Once, in Cleveland, I'd gone on a blind date with a friend of a colleague who thought we'd get along because of our Chicago connection. My date, who went only by the initial J, had told me about a restaurant she really liked in Logan Square but wouldn't give me the name of the place. When I pressed her, she'd said, "Honey, this place wasn't around back when you lived there."

"I go to Chicago all the time to visit my grandmother," I'd explained.

She had waved me off. "This is Logan Square, not Highland Park. It's completely changed since you moved. It's happening now."

"I've been to Logan Square many times." The neighborhood had changed—gentrified, mostly, so whether or not that counted as "happening" was up for debate. The idea that I didn't know that because I no longer lived in the city offended me.

"You wouldn't know this place. Honestly, it's like not even on any restaurant list. You basically have to know the chef to even know where it's located."

I had skipped dessert and coffee that night and never called J again.

Caroline's mind appeared to operate in a similar way. For daring to suggest I knew the train schedule, I had revealed myself to be an idiot out-of-towner who didn't know anything about the world, and my naivete was ruining her Christmas Eve.

Charlie dutifully got her phone back out. It took a minute for her to get the train schedule loaded, but once she had, she didn't have to tell me what she found. I could see on her face it wasn't good news.

"Nothing tonight? At all? How can that even be possible?"

"Not nothing," she said. "We have thirty minutes to catch the last train. Care, do you think you can get all the way downtown in thirty minutes?"

Caroline pursed her red lips again. She was going to get premature wrinkles if she kept that up. "I'm not going to break any laws."

"No one's asking you to."

"The traffic is awful."

"Just try to make it, okay? Dana really wants to get to her grandmother's house."

Oh, well, if Dana needs to get there, I imagined Caroline saying to herself. She didn't answer Charlie aloud.

We hit a yellow light, and Caroline accelerated through it.

A few blocks later, the GPS told us to turn right at a backed-up intersection, and Caroline took a shortcut through a gas station.

Maybe she really wanted to get me to the train station on time, though I doubted she cared that much about whether I got home to Nana. More likely, she wanted to please Charlie. Or maybe she just wanted to be done playing the role of our chauffeur. Either way, I appreciated her efforts.

We rode in silence. The old red brick buildings of the south side transitioned into the warehouse lofts of the South Loop and then the glass and steel skyscrapers of the Loop. As we drew closer to the train station, my heart began to beat a little more quickly. In my mind I was chanting, *Come on, come on, hurry,* as I watched the clock on the radio advance closer to 7:30. If we made it by then, I might be able to run to the platform in time to jump on the train. Maybe.

CHAPTER EIGHT

Caroline pulled up to the train station at 7:35 on the nose. I thought it was a lost cause, but Charlie pushed me out the door, yelling thanks to Caroline over her shoulder. Charlie grabbed my hand and pulled me into the station. We raced toward the platforms, pausing only for a second to read the signs before Charlie yanked me in the right direction.

We were nearly to platform thirteen when we stopped cold. The platform was empty. I could see the train making its way onto the merged tracks that led out of the Loop and northbound.

Clenching my fists, I let out a combination of a groan and a scream. "Is this a joke? Is this a cosmic joke? What are we supposed to do now?" I paced in a circle. "Okay, think, Dana, think. You know what? I'll call a cab. I'll just take a cab the whole way."

"Do you know how much money that'll cost?"

"Do you think I care? My grandmother is waiting for me. On Christmas Eve."

"Dana, all your stuff is in my truck—your purse, your phone, your suitcase with your clothes—"

"Yeah, and why is that? Because you insisted on getting off the highway, when I told you not to, and then you had to take that turn that led us to the street where the accident happened, and we could have just veered around it, but you insisted on getting out to help them and you didn't even park your car legally."

"What are you saying, Dana?" Charlie's eyes looked cold.

"I'm saying this is all your fault. This whole stupid day is your fault."

"I didn't make your car break down. I didn't make you ride with me."

"Yes, you did!" I laughed. "You pretty much did exactly that. You kept reminding me how cold it was and how there was no other way to get here. I was looking up car rental services when you showed up at that diner. I could have done that, or I could have taken the train from Indiana."

"It doesn't go all the way to Elkhart," Charlie said. "You'd still have needed a ride to—"

"Shut up, just shut up!"

I didn't want Charlie to be rational, and I didn't want to hear her explain how the day might have gone differently if I'd made different choices. Honestly, what other choices could I have made? I hadn't even known I was in Elkhart. Wherever Elkhart is. Charlie swooped in and promised me she'd rescue me, and I'd trusted her because I was attracted to her and because I wanted someone else to clean up my mess.

And look what that had gotten me. I'd believed Charlie would make everything better. Instead, she had done nothing but fail at that promise ever since I got into her truck. I could have sat in my car on the interstate until the highway patrol came. Or called roadside assistance back at the diner and had them take me to a car rental service. There were a million other possibilities for how this day could have gone, all of which had been erased because I'd put my trust in Charlie.

"I would have been better off without your help!" I started walking toward the main exit.

I could hear Charlie trailing behind me, calling my name. I didn't know where I was going to go without a wallet or phone or car, but I knew I didn't want to be around her anymore.

As I pushed past the food court, a crowd of people swallowed me, drowning the sound of Charlie's voice. I was carried with the crowd all the way to the main lobby, but I stopped before letting myself get pushed out the giant set of revolving doors. I couldn't face going back out into the cold night without a plan. I found an empty bench, sat down, and started crying.

A few minutes later, a paper napkin appeared in front of my face. I accepted it readily and wiped away my tears and snot. Then there was a chocolate frosted donut. I looked up.

Charlie was holding the donut out as a peace offering. Her eyes looked earnest and worried. She tipped her head toward the empty space next to me, asking if she could sit, and I nodded. She broke the donut in half and ate a bite.

"Gimme," I choked, reaching for the other half.

"I'm sorry," she said gently. "I'm really sorry everything has gotten so screwed up today. I really thought I was helping you."

"I know." The donut tasted sickly sweet but fluffy and comforting. "I'm sorry for what I said. I appreciate everything you've tried to do, really. I was totally stranded in Indiana, and I just wanted someone to solve the problem for me, and you did."

"Not very well. I shouldn't have gotten off the highway. You were so fidgety, and I think…" Charlie scrunched up her face. "Honestly, I think I wanted to impress you by showing you I could take a different route."

"That backfired."

"You could say."

I ate the rest of my donut half. "You were awesome with the people in that accident. I don't know if someone else would have gotten out and helped them like that. Maybe there was a reason we made that turn."

Charlie seemed to recognize the gift I was giving her, and she threw back her own. "It's made it that much harder for you to get home."

"Eh, we made it this far. Only twenty-five more miles." I looked at her. Her brown eyes were pools of empathy. I wanted to hold her hand or lean my head on her shoulder, but I couldn't. I didn't really know what her relationship with Caroline was or why she wasn't freaking out about getting to her own family. I didn't know why she had jumped out of the car to make sure I got on the train. Had she been planning to take a train, too? The train to Deerfield was on a different line with a different schedule, and while we were running through the station, we hadn't bothered to check the schedule for her train. There was a lot I didn't know about Charlie, and I hadn't bothered asking because I'd been so absorbed with my own predicament.

And yet, I heard myself putting my trust in her once again and asking, "What do we do now?"

"Now...now we finish this donut," Charlie suggested.

"How have you not finished that yet?" I reached over and tore a piece from her half and crammed it in my mouth before she could stop me. Charlie gestured to the corner of my mouth, and I tried to wipe away whatever chocolate frosting had found its home there. Apparently, I missed. With a gentle thumb, she rubbed my lip, and I felt her touch warm every crevice of my body. It took all my willpower not to suck on her thumb.

"Now that the donut is gone," she suggested, "maybe we should get some coffee or something while we figure out what to do."

"I think it's extremely rude of you not to have provided coffee upfront." When I was little, I preferred to eat donuts with chocolate milk. Thinking of that now made my teeth feel corroded. Coffee was the only way to go with sweets.

"Completely uncivilized," Charlie agreed. "What was I thinking?" She tapped my knee. "Come with me. We'll get some now."

"I'm so worried about my Nana," I admitted. "I told her I'd be home at dinnertime, and she didn't answer her phone when I called earlier. And, of course, I don't know anyone else's number to call them. If I even had a phone with which to call in the first place."

"'With which to call'? Who talks like that?" Charlie handed her phone over to me.

I looked at it. It had a chunky black case, the kind that prevented breakage from elephants stomping on the device. I wondered if she got it because the pigs had cracked the screen with their heavy hooves. My own phone was also in a protective case, a hot pink one, but it was much slimmer. If I ever saw it again.

Without anyone's number, I could only think of getting in touch with Mitchell Wormerstein. He was the singular person who knew what was going on and why it was taking me so long to get to Highland Park. Maybe I'd luck out, and he'd be that rare twenty-first century creature whose phone number was actually posted on the internet. I tried searching for his name but mostly got very old results about his accomplishments in high school and college. He'd been on the track team. I would never have guessed, not from all the wheezing he'd done in junior high.

Next I tried to search for Mitch Stein, but there were too many results for me to figure out which ones actually referred to the person I was looking for.

"Try Facebook," Charlie suggested. "If you find his profile, you can send him a direct message."

"But it's logged in under you."

"That's okay. I don't mind if you use it. You can explain to him that it's you."

It wasn't as hard to identify the right Mitch Stein on Facebook, since there was a profile picture attached. Although the photo was of a thirtysomething man, I recognized the facial features enough to know it was the same guy. My suspicions about his ugly duckling transformation were confirmed. Somewhere between eighth grade and age thirty, Mitch had blossomed into a very handsome man. His profile said he lived in California, and I thought with envy for a moment about his beaches and palm trees compared to my icy shores of Lake Erie in the winter. I used Charlie's log-in to explain the situation in a lengthy and probably neurotic message.

"Can I give him your phone number? In case he needs to call?"

Charlie dutifully recited her number while I typed into the tiny text box. I hoped that I'd hear from him soon but doubted it, since messages from non-friends were very easy to ignore on the platform. Plus, if Ruthie's family gathering was in full swing, what were the odds Mitchell was even checking his messages? Still, I had reached out to him, and under the circumstances, that was probably the best I could do.

Now it was time to turn my attention back to the more pressing matter of transportation. When we had first arrived at the station, there had been a row of cabs awaiting passengers out front. I could see through the tinted glass windows of the lobby that the peak cab time had passed. If we wanted a cab, we'd have to go up the street to a different intersection and try our luck, or we'd have to call one directly. I no longer had an Uber account, since I'd deleted it in a fit of solidarity with drivers over their working conditions a few years earlier, and then I'd stupidly deleted my PayPal account. I had regretted my hasty ethics when my designated driver friend took off with some random guy one Saturday night and left me to figure out how to get home from a bar that was miles from my apartment. Charlie didn't seem like the type to have ride share apps on her phone. If she had, why would she have bothered calling Caroline? I supposed I could persuade her to download one and open a new account, but that seemed like a giant hassle. And on Christmas Eve, there would be a ridiculous surcharge.

I knew from some wild, drunken escapades when I was younger that I could take the El to the airport, and from there take an airport shuttle to Highland Park. It would take a lot longer. From downtown, the blue line train to O'Hare took nearly an hour, but it would be much cheaper than taking a cab the whole distance. If airport shuttles were even available without a reservation on Christmas Eve.

The question was whether I was more worried about getting home as fast as possible or about taking money from Charlie—assuming she'd loan me any at all.

The phone in my hand buzzed, and an unknown number with an 847 prefix popped up. "It's Mitch!" I told Charlie, jumping up from the bench. I moved a few paces away and answered. Faced with a real voice on the other end, I went hysterical. "Mitch, it's Dana! Is my Nana okay?!"

"She's fine," he assured me. "We saw your message, so Granny went over to get her. We just finished dinner, but we have plenty of leftovers in case she hasn't eaten."

"She needs her pills. They're due at eight thirty."

"I'll call Granny when we hang up and have her remind Mrs. Gottfried. Is there anything else you want us to check on?"

I glanced over at Charlie, suddenly unsure how to explain this nightmare of a day to a virtual stranger like Mitchell Wormerstein. How much did I want him to know, and how much would he tell Nana? How much did I want Nana to know, and how much could we avoid telling her to spare her the unnecessary worry? Maybe more importantly, how stupid would the whole story make me look? After all, I was the one who didn't know how to take care of her car and had let it go *kaput*. I was the one who foolishly got in the car with not one but two strangers. Would Mitchell even believe the part about the car accident and the tow truck, or would he and his family think the whole crazy adventure had been some excuse to spend time with a random hot person I'd stumbled across along the drive home?

"At this point, I'm not even sure how I'm going to get there tonight."

"Are you all right?"

"Yeah, it's nothing like that. I told you my car died? Well, I've been bumming a ride, but then that car ran into some trouble, and I missed the train, and…here we are. Would you mind keeping me posted on Nana? You can call me at this number if you need to. For a while, anyway." I assumed that Charlie and I would go our separate ways at some point, maybe even soon, but it was reassuring to think of Mitchell being able to contact me if he needed to.

"You know, Dana, it's not really my place, but doesn't your grandmother take care of herself the rest of the year when you're not here?"

He had a good point. She did. Sort of. I didn't worry any less when I was in Cleveland, but the distance certainly meant that sometimes Nana wasn't foremost on my mind. I hated that. I felt like a terrible granddaughter, but it was the reality of the situation. Usually, the closer I got to Nana physically, the more I panicked about her health and safety. Somewhere in the deep recesses of my brain, I probably suspected it was out of fear that one day, I'd be driving to her, and it would be too late. That was partly what had motivated me to quit my job. I wanted to move so that if something serious happened to Nana, I would be nearby.

Of course, partly I had been motivated by the impending sense that my boss, Karen, an egomaniacal woman of about sixty, was going to fire me at any second because I had pissed off one of our wealthy donors at a benefit. He'd said something nasty about the migrant workforce, and I hadn't held my tongue the way I was supposed to. There was a script to these things. People like me, low on the office ladder, weren't supposed to tell off people like him, millionaires who felt they could do and say what they wanted. Women weren't supposed to tell off men. Thirty-two-year-olds weren't supposed to tell off people old enough to be their parents. Any way you stacked it, I was out of line, and I knew that after Karen heard about it, I'd be gone. I had beaten her to the punch, so I wouldn't have to report that I'd been terminated on every future job application.

"I don't like letting her down," I said to Mitch. "You'll keep her company?"

"Absolutely. We have plans for hot chocolate and games in a little bit."

I pictured his family in matching plaid pajamas, gathered in front of the fireplace with mugs topped with mountains of mini marshmallows. Laughing and playing Yahtzee. Or maybe Scattergories. Like something out of a clothing catalog.

"How does Ruthie feel about that?"

"She's fine with the hot chocolate, though there has been some arguing about whether or not it should have peppermint liqueur added."

"Nana will definitely be pro-liqueur. She's not supposed to drink with her medication, but she always does."

"Granny's the same. There's only so much we can tell them about how to live their lives."

Talking to Mitchell made me a little less anxious. Something about his voice made me believe that he would take good care of Nana. I already knew Ruthie and her kids would look out for her, but having someone my age who understood was reassuring. "Listen, Mitch, if I can't get there tonight—"

"It sounds like you're having a rough day. Just take care of yourself, and we'll make sure Mrs. Gottfried is entertained and well rested for when you do arrive."

My heart felt a million times lighter. "Thank you. I mean it. Thank you so much."

When I returned to the bench, Charlie was brooding in contrast to my newly improved mood. I gave her back the phone but warned that Mitch might call again.

"I guess we should get you that cab," she said, standing as I sat down.

"Cab?" I trailed after her. We pushed through the revolving door and back into the frigid night air. Powdered sugar was sprinkling down from the sky. It was my favorite kind of snow, the kind that didn't stick and looked beautiful. It was like walking through a snow globe. Even without a coat, I couldn't help but admire how beautiful the night had become.

"Where are all the cabs?" Charlie groused. "Damn, it's cold out here."

"Gone. Last train came and went. We'll have to go somewhere else to get a cab now—that is, if you're willing to spot me the money for it..."

"We could ask Caroline to drive us to Highland Park." I wasn't sure if Charlie was suggesting it because it was better than loaning a virtual stranger a hundred dollars for a cab ride and probably never getting paid back or if she just missed Caroline in the half hour since we'd parted company.

My own thoughts were conflicted. I partly wished we'd asked Caroline to drive us the whole way as soon as we'd learned we couldn't get the car back from the city tow lot, but I hadn't been able to ask. It was Christmas Eve, and I assumed we had already inconvenienced her. So we'd gone on this futile quest to find a train. Asking Caroline to drive us to the suburbs now seemed like a ridiculously big favor to pile onto the previous one. If we took a cab, I would certainly find a way to pay back Charlie whatever money she was able to give me toward the fare. Or maybe I could use her phone to request one and pay in advance online. The cab option seemed more logical than asking Caroline to come back. Plus, Caroline hadn't exactly made our ride the most pleasant.

"I don't think Caroline liked me very much."

"Okay, listen, here's the thing." Charlie tugged gently on the sleeve of my shirt to make me turn toward her. "She might have been rude to you because I might have told her you're my girlfriend."

"You what?!"

In our few hours together, I'd seen Charlie compassionate, confident, and funny, but I had not seen the side of Charlie I was seeing at that moment. Nervous. Charlie was nervous that I would be angry at her. And with good reason.

"When I called her to come get us after the accident, I might have said I was with someone, and she might have asked if it was my new girlfriend, and I might have said yes."

"You *might* have done that?" Not that it wasn't flattering to be considered Charlie's girlfriend, but I didn't appreciate stories being told about me without my knowledge, especially not to someone whose lips were the color of the blood she drank for breakfast, someone who clearly disdained me but on whom I had to rely for help.

Charlie sighed. "Caroline is my ex."

That explained the faces she'd made, the looks she'd given us. Her snotty attitude. Caroline was jealous that Charlie had a new girlfriend. But why did Charlie care about making Caroline jealous in the first place?

"Were you using me to get her back? Hoping she'd be jealous if you said you had a girlfriend and throw herself at you or something?"

"What? No! I do *not* want to get back together with Caroline. That relationship was a train wreck."

"Then why do you care if she thinks you have a girlfriend?"

"She and the person she started dating after me moved in together, and I guess…" Charlie shrugged.

"You didn't want her to think she was winning the breakup." I shivered. "Can we go back inside?"

"Oh, Dane, you don't have a coat! I'm sorry. You want mine?"

Charlie's coat would not fit me. No way. Even though it was too big for her, she was pint-sized, and I was…wearing a few more pounds than I had in college. I definitely didn't want to try it on and get stuck with an arm not fitting in the sleeve or with the whole thing unable to wrap around my body. While I appreciated the chivalry of the offer, I was too embarrassed to explain why I had to decline it.

"Let's get you inside," Charlie suggested.

We walked away from the empty cab stand to the main lobby doors, but as I threw my body against one, it didn't give. My forehead knocked against the glass.

"The doors are locked," Charlie mused.

Through the glass I could see that the escalator wasn't moving. The train station was closed. Of course. The last train had come and gone, the food courts had shut down for the night, and now the station itself was locked until morning when the first train arrived, whatever time that might be on a holiday.

Charlie and I were stuck.

CHAPTER NINE

"What do we do now?"

Charlie offered her coat again, and this time I didn't protest. I didn't know if she sensed that it wouldn't fit or didn't want the inconvenience of fully helping me into it, but she draped it over my shoulders like a cloak. With my arms out of the sleeves, I was able to get the zipper started enough to keep the coat in place. It gave me a little warmth, but Charlie was now only wearing a red flannel shirt with the sleeve cuffs turned up. She'd need the coat back soon enough.

"Now I guess we walk."

Charlie held out her hand, and I took it. As we headed east toward a more populated part of downtown, the fake movie snow became a freezing drizzle. I squinted my eyes against it and wished I had a hat. If the cold wetness bothered Charlie, she didn't react. She kept my hand in her gloved palm, and although it wasn't exactly romantic hand-holding with fingers laced together, it was comforting. It reminded me that I wasn't alone on this journey.

A few blocks to the east and north, closer to the river and Michigan Avenue, we found a restaurant that catered to tourists. Despite the fact that it was Christmas Eve, it was open and quite crowded inside. We didn't bother checking in with the host, since it was obvious from the throng of people in the vestibule that there was a long wait for a table. We headed to the spacious bar. There was one open seat, which Charlie let me take. She leaned her arm on the back of the stool, and her breath tickled my neck.

"I don't have any money," I reminded her. I assumed she was willing to buy me something to eat, since she had suggested going into the restaurant. But now that we were seated and looking at the massively oversized and overpriced menu, I wondered once again what her financial situation was. Her truck was rusty, and her clothes were the simple clothes of a farmer, out of place in this big, bright space. And yet her house had an espresso machine, and she had previously dated a glamour girl who drove a BMW.

"It's okay," she said. "Anything you want."

I skimmed the laminated menu I was holding. I doubted Charlie really meant it, and I didn't want to commit to ordering something that would take an hour to cook and eat. This pit stop was just supposed to get us out of the rain and give us a chance to recharge while we figured out our next move.

"Do you want to split something?" I asked.

"Sure, what were you thinking?"

Actually, I was thinking that I wanted to gorge on a sloppy cheeseburger by myself, but certain things were not done in front of attractive strangers. Plus, the menu didn't even specify if it came with fries. What would be the point of a cheeseburger in that case? I flipped to the appetizer page, trying to figure out what Charlie might like. Chicken wontons? Chicken was usually a safe bet, right? Everybody liked chicken. Maybe the chicken quesadilla? I suggested it out loud.

"Actually, I'm vegan. Sorry, I should have said that first."

"Oh, yeah, you told me that, like, ninety miles ago."

"Sorry, it can be kind of hard to order at places like this. If you want to get something on your own..."

"No, no, it's fine." It wasn't fine at all. I needed some real sustenance, and I was staring at a laminated menu full of options with meat and bacon and cheese. Honestly, at that point, I would have happily eaten all three at the same time.

When the bartender made his way to our end of the bar, I ordered the hummus plate.

"Not exactly how you thought you'd be spending Christmas Eve, huh?" Charlie said.

"Not even close." I looked over my shoulder at her. She'd been so worried about me and Nana, but what about her own family? Were they waiting for her, or did they still think she was coming the following day?

"Have you called your family in all of this?"

"I texted. To be honest, I don't think they'll care too much."

"They won't?"

I still didn't know anything about her family, but I wanted to. I hoped Charlie would be willing to open up a little, as she had with the revelation about her past relationship with Caroline. I tended to be an oversharer, emotionally slutty, telling stories about my past to the cashier at Whole Foods, but recently, I'd started to notice how hard it was for some people to do likewise. And I'd begun to appreciate what a gift it was when they did.

Charlie reached around me for the giant glass of water that was resting on the bar. Her body brushed against mine. I couldn't feel anything because she was once again wearing the bulky coat, but the physical contact nevertheless sent a shiver through me. "My folks and I don't get along that well. I guess I didn't turn out the way they expected."

"You mean because you're gay—uh, queer—I mean, genderqueer?"

Smooth, Dana.

"Maybe. Maybe because I want to do something meaningful with my life instead of making a lot of money for the sake of having it. Maybe because I broke up with Caroline, I don't know."

Since she had broached the subject, I felt I could ask a follow-up. "What happened between you? She obviously must care if she was willing to come pick you up out of the blue on Christmas Eve."

"She's just….we were just…"

Charlie had a tendency to look down when she was trying to express complex thoughts, and I noticed she did it now. I thought I'd let her off the hook.

"Sometimes things just don't work out," I supplied.

"Yeah."

When the hummus plate arrived, I moved my barstool to face Charlie, and we ate off my lap. After a few minutes of chewing in silence, I felt refreshed enough to figure out what our next move was going to be.

We went through a couple of options. We talked about asking someone from one of our families to drive down and get us, but Charlie seemed less enthused about that option. The only person I knew to call was Mitchell Wormerstein, but he'd flown into town. I didn't know if he could get access to a car or if he'd even be willing to come. Our entire relationship consisted of a few phone calls and a Facebook message under someone else's name, so it probably wasn't a good idea to ask him for a two-hour favor. Besides, if Mitchell left his family's Christmas Eve party, Nana would know something was up with me, and I didn't want her to worry.

Another possibility was sending me on my way while Charlie stayed behind, maybe asking Caroline if she could crash with her, until she could either take the train home or, if she waited another day, get the truck out of the tow lot. I didn't like that option very much, since it would still take forever and cost a fortune and since it meant leaving Charlie with Caroline. I also didn't think Charlie should miss time with her family, even if they had a lot of issues to work out. Or, and this was the option I disliked the most, we could both stay at Caroline's, since it was getting so late. In the morning, we could take the first train together. There was no way we'd find a hotel on Christmas Eve. Crashing at Caroline's made the most sense logistically, but I wouldn't really entertain it. Even if Caroline thought we were a couple and put us in the same guest bedroom—which was a little tempting—I had to take a hard pass on the idea of having to deal with her again.

There was the earlier thought I'd had of taking a ride share or licensed cab all the way to Highland Park and Deerfield. I mentioned it casually, and Charlie, ever the knight in shining armor, downloaded an app, created an account, and tried to order a ride.

"It says the wait time is four hours, and the estimated cost is two hundred and fifty dollars."

Charlie was careful to keep a neutral tone, but I sensed the money was a problem.

"Cancel that shit," I said. "We can walk faster."

Charlie looked relieved. She fessed up that she wasn't flush with cash and that her one credit card was probably close to its limit. This confirmed my suspicions about her financial situation, though I had to wonder about what led to it. Deerfield wasn't exactly a working-class suburb, and that house in the woods was hardly a slum.

"Here's the thing," she said, "and you are one of exactly two people in the world who know this, so I hope you'll act cool after I tell you."

It meant a lot to me that she would trust me with whatever she was about to say, that she already had that kind of confidence in me. "No judgment," I swore. "You can talk to me."

"My parents refused to pay for college after I told them I was attracted to women, so I took out a bunch of loans. And then I paid for graduate school with more loans. When I told them I'm genderqueer, they completely cut me off. Now I'm not in school anymore, and the loan payments are due, plus interest. I make a reasonable enough income for where I live, but when you combine it with all the loan payments, I'm pretty strapped."

The carrot stick I was chewing clumped in my throat, refusing to be swallowed. I blinked back a few tears of outrage on Charlie's behalf. Her economic circumstances had been a result of her gender and sexuality, something she had no control over. Plenty of parents didn't pay for their children's college—sometimes for valid reasons—but who would cut their child off financially for something as inconsequential as which gender they wanted to date and what clothes they wanted to wear?

"How do your parents feel about you being trans now?"

"Genderqueer," Charlie corrected me. I wondered what the distinction was, but this wasn't the moment to ask. "They won't use anything but 'she' pronouns, and they insist on calling me Charlotte instead of Charlie, which is stupid because when I was little, everyone called me Charlie anyway."

"Charlie's your real name?" I had assumed it was something Charlie chose for herself.

"Dana, whether my parents gave it to me or I picked it, it would be my real name."

It was a gentle correction, but I felt chastened nonetheless. "Of course. My mistake." I wanted to change the subject away from me. "Have your parents ever met your girlfriends?"

"They liked Caroline because she was…well, she doesn't wear steel-toe boots and play with pigs all day."

Caroline was femme. And posh.

"Was she from Deerfield, too? How did you meet?"

"We met in college, but we didn't date until afterward. It was because of her that I started going to my parents' house for things like holidays."

I wanted to ask how the cool, reserved person I'd met in the car was the same person who had brought Charlie back to the family fold, but I wasn't sure how far I could push and how much more Charlie was willing to give me. I didn't want to waste all my questions on Caroline.

"Is this going to be the first time you're going to your family's house without her?"

"No, we broke up before Christmas last year, so I did that alone."

They'd broken up a year ago, yet they were still in touch and competing to see whose life had turned out better. I filed this information away for later use.

"What made you want to keep in touch with your family at all? Is that okay to ask?"

"Yeah, it's cool." She shrugged and reached around me again for her water. I was facing her this time, and I could feel her breath as she leaned past. It wasn't hard to fantasize about kissing her soft pink lips.

Charlie obviously had other thoughts on her mind. "Care, though, I know she seems like a total brat, but she has a good enough heart."

Nothing says, "I'm fantasizing about kissing you," like mentioning an ex. Between her frequent suggestions that we rely on Caroline to rescue us and her lie to Caroline that she and I were dating, I had to accept that Charlie was still carrying a torch. Even if she couldn't admit it to me—or herself.

I resigned myself to asking directly about the matter to clear the air.

"What makes you stay in touch with Caroline?" I wanted to hear Charlie say it was because they were in the process of divesting their joint assets or something. Charlie had a rare blood disorder, and Caroline was the only person who could supply transfusions. Something that indicated their continued communication wasn't what I suspected. But I knew it was.

"Honestly, we don't have much in common. We never did. I know she can be kind of…difficult, and she clearly likes showing off how much better her life has gone since we broke up. That's how I knew she'd come get us. Any chance to make me feel dependent on her generosity, she'll take. I get what you're probably thinking right now, but I'm telling you, I've known her for years, and she's—oh, hey, she's actually calling right now."

I swiveled my barstool back around to give her the illusion of privacy while she talked. I dredged the last piece of pita through the garlicky hummus. No kissing tonight for me. My breath was probably lethal.

"Dana?" Charlie said quietly. "I'm just going to step outside."

And it wasn't exactly as if I was with someone who wanted to kiss me. I watched Charlie go outside and felt my heart sink. I was certain we'd had a spark between us, but clearly that meant nothing in the face of a great former love.

I'd never had a Caroline, so maybe I couldn't understand. It wasn't as if I was a virgin or some total loner. In college I'd had a few girlfriends, and I knew my way around a dating app as an adult. I had friends in Cleveland—a few, anyway—okay, like two, but they were good, reliable friends. Whom I had only known for a total of two years. Compared to Charlie, my life was a string of short-term interactions. Even my relationship with my parents hadn't survived. I'm not exactly sure how it could have, since they were dead, but it felt like a fitting example of how fleeting my connections with people tended to be. Charlie was just another one of those fleeting connections. At least I'd had those few hours of riding in the car with someone else, as I'd always pictured.

Now it would be back to me and Nana. We should have probably gotten a dog or something. If it were going to be the two of us, if Nana were my only meaningful connection, then I wanted to get to her as quickly as possible and appreciate the time I had left with her.

The bartender eventually set the bill in front of me. Fifteen dollars for a dollop of hummus, two pitas, some carrot sticks, and two glasses of water. A week before, I'd have slapped down a credit card without even checking the bill. Now, with my employment situation a little less than ideal, the price made me cringe. I hoped Charlie was okay with it. If she could cover the bill, I would make it up to her and then some once we got my purse back from her truck. I suspected, though, that after sitting on the bench seat in plain sight for two days, my purse and phone would be mysteriously gone when the truck was finally rescued from the tow lot. Of course, Charlie wouldn't have to wait that long for reimbursement. I could have Nana front her. I might have been broke and facing purse theft, but Nana had plenty of money.

Charlie came back in and took care of the bill without commenting on the total. "Caroline is going to take you to Highland Park tonight."

Apparently, I didn't get a say in the matter. "Are you going to come with me?"

"That's fine."

When someone used the expression "that's fine," it usually meant the opposite. I became irritated at Charlie's abrupt change of mood. "Aren't you going to your family's house tonight?"

"I don't know, it's getting kind of late."

"You're avoiding them."

"I didn't say that. I'm not even thinking about myself right now. I'm trying to figure out how to get you home, and I'm offering to come with you if you don't feel comfortable being in the car alone with Caroline."

"So, if I go with Caroline, and you come with us because Caroline hates me because she thinks I'm your girlfriend, then you're going to drive all the way back with her? And...sleep on her couch?"

Or sleep with her.

Charlie was vexed at my questions. "I have other friends. Not that it's any of your business."

"Considering I'm your fake girlfriend, it's kind of my business."

She looked at me in disbelief, but I stared back. She was the one who'd lied to Caroline, after all. If she now planned to rekindle their relationship, she'd have to remember what she'd said and figure out how to explain it.

"What about your family?" I added for good measure. "Did you tell them you were coming a day earlier?"

"Dana, please don't push me." She was looking away again. "I've got to deal with my family on my own time and under my own circumstances."

"Do you even plan to find a way to get to Deerfield tomorrow?" Her silence spoke volumes. "Charlie, you drove all this way! You have to see them!"

"Caroline is meeting us a few blocks away where it'll be easier to find us," she informed me. "We should go."

I frowned as I slid off my stool and followed her out of the restaurant.

Charlie didn't say a word while we walked a few blocks to a more convenient location for Caroline to pick us up. I didn't press her. It wasn't going to be the last time I saw her, since I'd have to figure out how to get my stuff out of the truck. But there was a definite shift in the mood. Before, even when I was shouting at her about getting off the highway, it had felt as if we were in the adventure together. Now I felt lonely. I just wanted to get home, and I honestly didn't care if Charlie came or not.

When Caroline arrived, Charlie got in the front seat. I took my place immediately behind her, where I couldn't hear anything she and Caroline said to each other. After a few blocks, though, I could tell they were fighting, and I strained to hear them over the noises of the highway and the heat blowers. After a few minutes of ignoring my existence, Charlie craned her neck around and shouted into the back seat, "Can you believe that?"

"Sorry, I couldn't hear anything."

She punched the radio off and lowered the heat. "Caroline just left a party."

My eyes widened. What a mess I had made of everyone's day. First, Charlie was taken off course and off schedule, and her truck had been towed, and now Caroline had had to leave her own party. Why hadn't we anticipated that? It was Christmas Eve. Naturally she had people to be spending it with. Why had she volunteered to drive me in that case?

"I'm only asking for an hour, Charlie," she snapped.

I was confused. Asking for an hour for what? We were the ones asking for an hour of her time to drive us north.

Nobody bothered explaining to me, but Charlie nonetheless made it clear what was going on. "Caroline, I am *not* going to pretend we're still together. You should have told them the truth."

"I don't understand why you won't do it," Caroline retorted. "It's really not that big of a deal, and you owe me for everything I've done for you. All you have to do is show up and drink a glass of wine and not say anything."

"You were supposed to drive Dana home!"

"And I will." Caroline smiled fiendishly. Her crimson lipstick was applied as thickly as it had been when she'd left us some hours ago. "As soon as you pretend to be my girlfriend."

CHAPTER TEN

From the back seat, I rolled my eyes. I shouldn't have expected Caroline to be willing to drive me all the way to Highland Park without wanting something in return. This meant more delays in getting to Nana's house. It was nearly Nana's bedtime. I had the code to her garage door, so I could get inside the house even if she was asleep, but if I woke her in the middle of the night, she'd be completely scared there was an intruder.

I resolved that at the next available moment, I would steal Charlie's phone away from her and call a licensed cab that I could pay with cash. Nana used to keep a stash of emergency money. Maybe she still did. I could ask the driver to wait while I went inside the house to find it. I could pay Nana back later. As soon as we got to Caroline's house, I was going to escape my captors and their ex drama.

The problem with my plan was that it took a long time to get to Caroline's house. She lived west in a suburb called Oak Park, the kind of suburb that wasn't altogether that different from the more residential parts of the city. Instead of half-acre lots with tree-lined streets, there were mid-rises and tightly clustered bungalows. The green and blue lines served Oak Park, so many people commuted from there to the Loop for work. It wasn't that far on a map, but in Chicago cross-town traffic, it was a slow, long drive. And it meant we were going in the wrong direction to get me home.

Caroline took us to a nondescript four-story red brick building off Augusta Boulevard. We parked in a numbered space in the lot in the back and went in through a heavy metal back door. Garish fluorescent lighting flooded the industrial-tiled path to another door, which took us to a cozily lit lobby with ornate moldings and Louis XIV-style chairs. With a perfectly manicured finger, Caroline stabbed the elevator button, and we waited, all glum for different reasons, until it dinged its arrival.

Inside the elevator, Caroline pushed the button for the top floor. Once the doors closed, Charlie came back to life. "I am not doing this," she repeated.

"You owe me," Caroline reminded her again, and I wondered if she meant for the rides today, or if there had been some larger unresolved matter between them.

"I can't pretend to be dating you. I can't do that to Dana."

"It's really not a big deal." Caroline turned to me, and the look in her eyes made it clear I was not allowed to disagree with her. "Right, Dana?"

"Um…"

"Charlie should simply act like we are still together for an hour, and then they can go home to you."

They. Caroline called Charlie "they." Was that part of what Charlie liked about her? Maybe she mistook appreciation that Caroline was sensitive to her identity for a continued romantic interest in her. If Charlie's parents had rejected her, I could see how Caroline's support would be attractive.

"Besides," Caroline continued, "you can't have been together that long. How serious is it really?"

"Care," Charlie warned her.

Caroline didn't pay any attention to Charlie. She and I locked gazes, two willful women who did not like each other and knew it. We were connected by this other person we both so clearly did like. I could see in her eyes that she didn't believe Charlie and I were in a relationship. She was goading me into admitting it. In that moment, I wondered if she even wanted Charlie back. I thought it was more likely that she was the kind of person who wanted things she couldn't have. The harder something was to get, the more she probably wanted it.

I could see her as the kind of person who didn't confess to her breakups, even though the one with Charlie had happened a year before. Caroline wasn't the type to admit to her failures. She could save face by having Charlie pretend they were still dating, and if she could humiliate Charlie a little in the process, so much the better.

"I thought you just moved in with your new girlfriend," I said.

Charlie bit her lip, and I could see her resisting the urge to laugh out loud. I hadn't meant the question to humiliate Caroline. Honestly. I was just confused about the situation and hadn't been given the full exposition. If my question embarrassed Caroline in the meantime, I supposed that was fine.

She made the face of someone who had sucked on a lemon. "It didn't work out," was all she'd say. She seemed to remember she had the upper hand. "Charlie has volunteered me to drive you to Highland Park tonight, on Christmas Eve, in the middle of my own party, so of course you wouldn't mind this gesture on their behalf as recompense."

I thought about how easygoing Charlie was and wondered how she'd ever gotten into a relationship with such a manipulative creature. When the accident happened, Charlie hadn't hesitated to jump out of the truck to check on the drivers. When we'd arrived at the train station, she'd pulled me to the platform to catch my train. She hadn't done any of those things because they benefited her. In fact, everything she had done today to help me had cost her something—time, money, social interactions—but she had done it because Charlie was a fundamentally generous person.

Not true for Caroline, who struck me as the type who would only help someone if it would also help her. I didn't like her very much.

"You don't mind, do you, Dana?" she pressed once more. "And then I'll drive you home."

That was her mistake. Regardless of how Charlie might have still been foolishly under her spell, I was not. Caroline thought she had me backed into a corner. If I wanted her to drive me home, I could not say no to her. What Caroline didn't realize was that I didn't take kindly to threats. When I was given an ultimatum, I never took it.

"Honestly, I just don't think anyone would believe the two of you are together," I said smoothly, reaching for Charlie, "since I can't keep my hands off this one."

Charlie gaped for a second before catching on. I put my arms around her from behind, her smaller frame nestled against mine, and smiled tartly at Caroline.

The elevator dinged open. Caroline's eyes narrowed, and her jaw set. She marched into the hall ahead of us. She was wearing a pair of red heels that matched her lipstick, but she teetered in them, and that tiny glimpse of her vulnerability gave me great pleasure.

As we followed her to her door, Charlie mouthed her thanks at me, and I nodded.

Caroline's condo was lit with candles and smelled of mulling spices. The other guests were gathered in the living room, which was open to the kitchen with its wide granite countertop and gleaming stainless steel appliances.

"You're back!" someone said enthusiastically. "We were about to open another bottle of champagne."

"Oh, yes, let's," Caroline agreed. Someone produced a bottle of Veuve Clicquot and opened it with the careful patience of a professional. The bottle made a satisfying *ffftt* as the cork slid gracefully from its neck. "Look who I brought, everyone. Charlie's finally arrived."

"Hello," Charlie greeted the group tepidly.

A man in a baby blue cashmere sweater came forward and enveloped Charlie in a bear hug. "We've been waiting for you all night!"

"I told them you had to work late and wouldn't be here on time," Caroline explained.

She was letting her friends continue to think they were dating. What a phony. Charlie wasn't even supposed to be in Chicago today. She had told me she was planning to drive up tomorrow.

The man in the blue cashmere turned to me with a wide smile. "And who is this?" he drawled. He was one of those people that, back when it was still socially acceptable to pronounce such judgments, I'd have said pinged my gaydar.

I seized my chance to intervene in the narrative. "Hi, I'm Dana." I offered my hand for a shake. "I guess there's been a little mix-up tonight because Charlie and I have been seeing each other for about two months, and she wanted me to meet all of you. But I think we may have completely forgotten our manners and neglected to tell Caroline I was coming!" I made a pouty face in Caroline's direction, like *Oops, my bad!*, matching her phoniness with my own.

"I'm Clint. It's nice to meet you." Then to Charlie, he said, as if I weren't able to hear, "She's cute."

Another well-mannered friend came forward to give me a small hug. "I'm Alyssa," she said to me. Then to Caroline, she added, "I don't understand. Did you and Charlie break up?"

Charlie managed to answer honestly. "Yes, we did." She spared Caroline the embarrassment of telling her friends how long ago they'd split and how long Caroline had been lying to them. "It was a friendly separation."

"Why didn't you tell us?" Alyssa asked. "You never said anything."

Caroline stammered something incoherent, and Charlie said something diplomatic about how things had been really busy, and they could never find the right time. I didn't think any of the party guests necessarily believed that answer, but they were mollified enough to leave the delicate situation alone in front of me, the new girlfriend. There would probably be a lot of texting about me later that night, I guessed.

"Dana, would you like a glass of champagne?" If Caroline couldn't pretend to have Charlie anymore, she was going to win her victory with magnanimity toward the other woman.

"Thank you." I matched her good manners with my own. "You have a lovely home."

As we settled into the living room, I took stock of our surroundings and our companions. They were not the bunch of friends I had expected, and once again I was reminded how little I truly knew about Charlie and how wrong my preconceptions tended to be. I had imagined bohemian artist types in one of those apartments in Pilsen with holes in the floorboards and no door on the bathroom. Instead, we were settled on an L-shaped gray suede sectional with champagne and a marble tray of cheese in front of us. Instead of dyed hair and piercings, Caroline and Charlie's mutual friends were clad in cashmere and silk. They were the kind of people I knew how to deal with because I'd grown up with people like them, and it was the kind of home I'd always felt comfortable in because I'd grown up affluent. I'd always assumed that as an adult, I'd live a similar life. While Nana kept my bank account padded with family money, I certainly didn't earn enough on my own to live the high life. I couldn't help envying Caroline a little.

The conversation was boring, mostly people catching up on gossip about other people I didn't know and didn't bother asking about. I drank my champagne and wondered how long I'd have to continue playing nice before I could get myself out of there. Eventually, though, Clint steered the conversation back to me.

"So tell us how you met." He drew out every syllable in a singsong voice.

Charlie and I looked at each other. I could tell she was struggling with this game, and I felt some sympathy that she was sitting in her ex-girlfriend's swank condo on Christmas Eve in her frayed jacket and work boots. She clearly didn't like lying and wasn't that good at it, and I appreciated that about her.

The sooner I played my role, the sooner I could get out of there and get home to Nana. Leaning my entire body against Charlie, I put one hand on the back of her neck, massaging gently, while the other hand came to rest on her thigh. I smiled as brightly as I could. "Do you know what an absolute angel you let slip away? I was stranded on the side of the highway in the snow, and Charlie came to rescue me."

When I took an improvisation workshop in college, we learned that the simplest way to invent a script on the fly was to stick as closely to the truth as possible. So far, I hadn't lied. That would make it easier to keep track of the story as the questions continued.

I could feel the muscles in Charlie's neck relax into my touch, even as she blushed.

"Well, that sounds romantic!" Clint screamed.

I met him decibel for decibel. "It was! She's been rescuing me ever since! A total Prince Charming. A real knight in shining armor."

"Oh my God, Dane," Charlie murmured almost imperceptibly.

I was laying it on a bit thick. I told myself to take it down a notch.

"So, Dana," Caroline asked, pouring another round of champagne, "what do you do for a living?" She made it to the blonde in a sapphire velvet dress to my left before she waved the bottle, showing it was empty. No refill for me.

I fumbled for a second. If these people knew Charlie, then they knew she lived in Indiana. I couldn't very well say that I worked in Cleveland.

"Dana's the lead researcher in the biosolids fertilizer division," Charlie supplied.

Now she was able to fabricate? And that's the best she could come up with? I groaned inwardly because this was straying from the rules of improvisation—to keep close to the truth—and because of all the fictional professions I could have been given, she had named one that was light years away from Caroline's glamour.

"Biosolids fertilizer?" the blonde asked.

"I work with shit," I translated.

Clint looked at me quizzically, but it didn't take him more than a second to put his high-wattage smile back on. "That sounds exciting!"

"It's actually cutting-edge research," Charlie told him. "Real high-profile stuff."

"And yet, you look so refined," Caroline said sharply. "I could never get Charlie to clean up, but look at you."

Look at me? I was wearing jeans and high-tops, not exactly the party frock she had on. My hair was in an efficient but unattractive ponytail. After being in the car for so long and then walking around in the rain and snow, my makeup was probably completely smeared. And although my gas station lunch had been hours before, my fingertips were still stained with the telltale signs of Cheetos. Even on my best days, I didn't look like a dream girlfriend, but this was another level.

"Dana used to compete in beauty pageants," Charlie announced.

If I had had any champagne left, I would have spit it out.

No one was going to believe that. I had a few extra pounds of curves, my face wasn't conventionally beautiful, and I couldn't remember the last time I put on a swimsuit.

But the lie had Charlie coming to life. I sat back against the suede couch and listened in horror as she spun out a fantasy version of my childhood.

"It's actually really funny. Dana's mom used to force her to do these baby pageants, you know, like you see on TV? But then when Dana was in high school, she started doing them all on her own, and she won a bunch. She had to quit when she went to college because she was too busy with homework, and she had to keep up her GPA for the scholarship she got from this organic agriculture company. She doesn't like to talk about it because she's too modest, but yeah. She has a few tiaras from winning and everything."

"Wow, Dana, I had no idea," Caroline deadpanned. She knew as well as I did that Charlie was lying.

"Um," I faltered. "Yeah. I—I just don't like to talk about it. It was a really long time ago."

"Don't be so modest," Charlie said. "Dana was Miss Teen Illinois 2001."

Clint sized me up again. I was certain he knew Charlie was lying. I made a little pleading face at him, asking him to let it be. He nodded silently and changed the topic of conversation.

I leaned toward Charlie. "I really need to get home."

"Will you excuse us for a second?" Charlie said to the group. She rose from the sofa, leaving me to follow her out of the living room down a short hallway. She opened a door to a small but impeccably tiled bathroom. She shut the door and turned on the fan. "Thank you so much for playing along."

"You're welcome."

"I couldn't deal with the idea of faking it with Caroline."

"Better to fake it with me then?" I crossed my arms over my chest. "What is all this about, anyway? Why didn't she tell your friends you had broken up? And why are you letting her manipulate you so much?" Charlie looked away. "Are you still carrying a torch for her?"

"What? No!"

"You told her I'm a shit-researching beauty queen!"

"So you're saying you're not having a good time?"

As much as I wanted to be angry, when I looked into Charlie's eyes, we both started laughing. "You owe me so big for that. So, so big. Honestly, who are these people even? How are these your friends? They seem so different from you."

"Caroline's friends, mostly. Clint and I have been friends since college, and he introduced me to everybody. He's good people."

"I gathered, but I don't like the way he keeps looking at me."

"He probably just can't figure out why I'm dating you," Charlie supplied. "You're very different from the women I usually date."

Considering that Caroline was rich and beautiful, I blinked a few times and told myself not to take it as an insult. "This is all very interesting information, but I just want to get to my grandmother's house. She's eighty-five, it's Christmas Eve, and I've had a really long day."

"Right, I'm sorry," Charlie said. "What do you need?"

"If you can let me use your phone, I'll call a cab."

"I thought you decided that would be too expensive."

"That was when I thought I'd have to borrow the money from you," I explained. "But I've thought it over, and I can tell the driver to wait while I get Nana's emergency cash stash. I don't think it'll be a big deal."

Charlie's face was neutral as she handed me her phone, and for a fleeting moment I wondered if she'd intentionally been dragging out our time together. Too bad, because I was about to put an end to this nightmarish journey once and for all.

I was trying to pull up phone numbers for cab companies when there was a soft tap on the bathroom door.

"It's me," a man's voice called.

Charlie opened the door, and Clint came in. "What's going on in here? Your absence is getting conspicuous." He looked at me. "Who are you, really? I know you're not their girlfriend."

"How do you know?" I was a little wounded. "I could be."

He frowned. "You keep calling them 'her,' for one thing."

"Clint," Charlie warned him.

"Honey, you told us more than a year ago you wanted to make that change, so I don't believe you'd date someone now who misgendered you." To me he added, "Did Charlie tell you they used to date Caroline?"

"She did, uh, they did, but it was screamingly obvious anyway."

"Caroline didn't like the change."

"Clint!" Charlie's warning was much less friendly that time.

What were the rules for such conversations, I wondered? Did Clint really have the right to talk to a random person like me about Charlie's gender identity? He didn't strike me as the inappropriate type. If anything, his willingness to play along with our terrible lies showed him to be a thoroughly sensitive and thoughtful person. Did that mean he knew it was okay to tell me these things about Charlie's past even if Charlie protested?

"I don't know if I'm comfortable having this conversation with you."

Clint smiled and put an arm around me. To Charlie he said, "I like her. She's good. Even if she keeps getting it wrong."

"She can call me whatever she wants," Charlie told him.

"Where did you find her?"

"She was telling the truth when she said I found her on the side of the road."

I bristled. "I am not a stray cat. Look, Clint, did you drive here? And how much money to convince you to drive me to Highland Park?"

"Highland Park?"

"Dana's trying to get to her grandmother's house. Her car broke down, so I was driving her, and then my car got towed."

"How did your car get towed if you were driving it?"

"Long story and very long night," Charlie said. "How about it, Clint? Drive us north?"

"I'd love to, hon, but I sold it to be more eco. I only walk or take the train now." He shook his head. "Let me tell you, that was a stupid thing to do in November."

"Can you borrow Caroline's?"

"I've been drinking all night, and you know she won't let either of us touch her keys." He sighed. "Let's order you a cab."

There was another knock, and we all looked at each other.

Even though the fan was on, Caroline's voice came floating through the door. "If you're all finished in there, some of us would like to use the room for its intended purpose."

"Honestly, Charlie, she's so awful," I whispered. "You really dated her?"

"She's not that bad." It sounded as if Charlie was trying to convince herself more than me.

"She's awful," Clint agreed. "But she's my sister, so we smile and make do." He turned off the fan and opened the door. "Okay, honey, it's all yours. That's what you get for eating too much fiber."

Caroline pushed past him into the room, where Charlie and I were still standing. "I hope everything is okay."

"Actually, yeah," Charlie replied, smiling devilishly. "Dana just surprised me with a proposal. We're getting married!"

CHAPTER ELEVEN

Forced to pretend she was happy for us, lest she seem as if she hadn't gotten over Charlie, Caroline opened another bottle of champagne, and the group toasted us. Some of them exchanged gifts with each other, an event I found incredibly awkward to sit through as the outsider. Eventually, our cab arrived, and Charlie and I said our good-byes to the party.

In the car, she pledged her gratitude over and over until I finally snapped at her to stop.

"I feel like you used me. And you lied to all those people."

"I'm sorry."

"Why did you do that?"

"It's complicated." Charlie tended to lower her voice when she felt shamed.

I, on the other hand, got loud. "What could possibly be so complicated? You told her about your identity, and she broke up with you. That was a year ago. So what?"

"I asked her to marry me."

I didn't have a response to that. I tried to picture Charlie in love with Caroline, the one rugged and deep, the other all gloss and surface. I couldn't imagine what that moment had looked like, when Charlie was so overcome with passion and commitment that she asked Caroline to spend their lives together.

"What happened?"

"She laughed at me."

"Oh, wow." In the darkness, I reached for her hand. "I'm so sorry."

"She said she didn't picture herself with someone like me."

Someone like Charlie. I wondered what Caroline meant by that. Was it Charlie's gender, as Clint had intimated before? Maybe Caroline had enjoyed their relationship until Charlie wanted to change pronouns, and that became too much for her? Or was "someone like Charlie" a reference to her pigs and boots and truck, compared to Caroline's slick BMW and condo?

The cynic in me thought "someone like Charlie" was a reference to Charlie's unfailingly kind heart, and, no, Caroline didn't deserve to spend her life with someone like that.

"Charlie, why on earth did you stay friends with her?"

She took her hand back. "We don't talk very often. It's just a connection to the city and the life I had here, I guess."

I looked over at her. She was looking down at her lap. "There's more, isn't there?"

"You're awfully perceptive for someone who just met me."

I shrugged. "I'm your fiancée. You're easy for me to read. So what's the real story?"

Charlie sighed. "After I told my parents, they didn't want much to do with me. If I thought telling them I liked girls was bad, this was…a lot worse. They'd always liked Clint and Caroline, though. Caroline fit into their world, and I thought, foolishly, that if I kept her in my life, maybe I could fit into their world, too."

I could empathize, but it also seemed that Charlie was using Caroline. If Caroline had a sense of that, no wonder she had such a lousy attitude.

"Why do you think Caroline stays in touch with you?" I asked. "What's in it for her?"

"Are you kidding? After she dumped me, it took about three weeks for her to call me and say she'd made a mistake. She's been begging me to take her back ever since."

That explained why Caroline wanted Charlie to pretend they were dating. Now that I had met Clint and the rest of her guests, though, I suspected no one would have been fooled by that deception. I remembered Charlie saying I wasn't her type, but then didn't most people date the wrong type until they found their true love, the one that broke the mold?

Not that I was suggesting I was Charlie's true love. But I definitely was more down-to-earth and, I hoped, a lot nicer than Caroline.

"She may be your type, but she's not right for you."

Charlie gave me a flirty smile in the darkness of the car. "What kind of person is right for me?"

My heart fluttered, but I knew Clint had felt I wasn't right either, for one very particular and very important reason. It was time to address it. "Has it bothered you today, me using 'she' pronouns? Clint said he knew I wasn't dating you because I did that."

"I love Clint, but he likes to stick his nose into places it doesn't belong."

"That doesn't answer my question."

"I told you that you can call me what you want, and I meant it."

"But wasn't that a big part of why you and Caroline—"

Charlie cut me off. "Some people get really upset about their pronouns. I respect that. I understand that. But I don't. To me it matters a lot more if someone understands me and a lot less that they call me something. With you..." Charlie cleared her—*their*—throat. "I feel like you respect what I've told you about who I am. Caroline didn't."

I didn't really know what I could say that would be meaningful, not just typical Dana trying to fill a silence with her prattling. Did I respect Charlie's identity? I thought I did. I didn't think I'd spent the day imagining Charlie as a woman. Had I? Those feminine features on their face and body were appealing, sure, but mostly because they were in such contrast to their more masculine qualities. I liked the balance. But did sexual attraction to Charlie's gender equate to respect for Charlie as a person? I didn't know for sure, but I did know that it mattered to me to get it right.

"You feel respected by me?"

"Do I have any reason not to?"

"I guess not. I just...I've been kind of fixated on getting home tonight, and I haven't really been thinking all that much about who you are."

"Now, see, that's my point."

After a few minutes, I changed the subject. "Clint is really Caroline's brother?"

"Yep."

"And your friend?"

"Used to be one of my best friends, actually. I miss him, but that's one of the sacrifices I made when I moved away." The wistful tone in their voice betrayed the matter-of-factness of their words.

"Do you miss living here?"

"I don't know. Sometimes. How about you?"

I wanted to tell them that I had quit my job and that this trip home was the start of a new life for me. I wanted to say that I felt I had tried really hard in Cleveland, but nothing had come of it. I had only a few friends, I barely dated, and I was profoundly lonely. I wanted to tell Charlie that I was the one with money troubles and that all my posturing about having money was because my family—not me—did. I wanted to admit everything to Charlie, yet something held me back.

Maybe I wasn't sure Charlie would understand. No, that was bullshit. Charlie's most defining quality so far had been empathy. Charlie would listen kindly, without judgment. So why didn't I tell them?

Because I didn't want them to stop being interested in me. Seeing behind the facade would definitely kill their interest.

If they had any interest in the first place.

Instead of saying any of the myriad, complicated thoughts tumbling around my brain about our time together and the connection I was pretty sure I had felt all night, I asked, "Clint really thought you and Caroline would be a good match?"

"Why are you fixated on me and Caroline?"

I blinked a few times. I wasn't fixated on them. I'd just been dealing with the fallout for the last four and a half hours.

"I mean," they continued, "I haven't asked you about your exes."

Why hadn't they? Were they more respectful of privacy than I was, or were they just not interested? Charlie had been giving me mixed signals all day. It was tiring. I had been on the road for nearly twelve hours, a huge portion of which had been spent with a total stranger that I foolishly thought I was getting to know. Maybe I wasn't. I could tell when Charlie felt remorseful or anxious, but other than that, did I really know Charlie? And did Charlie really know anything about me?

"There aren't any exes to tell you about."

My tone was pissy, and we both heard it. Charlie, though, ignored it as they said in that same sexy drawl that had gotten me into their truck in the first place, "Now see, darlin', I just can't believe that."

I let the compliment wash over me. I was worthy of being someone's girlfriend. I was loyal and funny and maybe I could never remember to charge my phone and I locked myself out at least once a month, but that didn't mean I was unworthy of love. Charlie could see it. Charlie could see what no one else had yet seen.

I bit my cheeks to keep from smiling.

We rode in silence until the cab driver reached our exit on the highway. To the east was Highland Park and Nana's house; to the west was Deerfield and Charlie's family.

The driver took the exit to the east. I could feel my excitement at finally getting to see Nana growing, but I knew that I'd feel the absence of not having Charlie by my side after we'd been through so much together.

When the driver stopped in front of the powder blue house with bright red door where Nana had lived for most of my life, I lingered in the cab with my hand on the car door handle. "I guess this is it."

"Yeah." Charlie ran a hand through their hair. "How long were you planning to be in town, anyway?"

The question reminded me that I had left a job, and I had little to return to. Still, I had exactly one week to be out of my apartment, so I couldn't really loiter in Chicago just because I'd made a new friend.

"Only two days."

I didn't know how I was going to get back to Cleveland without a car. I couldn't fly because I didn't have an ID. Maybe Nana could rent me a car, but I didn't think she had a valid driver's license anymore. I'd probably have to try to get an Illinois ID after the holiday, assuming Nana had my birth certificate and things, if I wanted to fly. Otherwise, I'd have to wait for Charlie to get the truck out of the tow lot, which would give me a purse with a license and two credit cards but still no mode of transportation of my own. Assuming the purse hadn't been stolen.

"Your purse and suitcase," Charlie reminded me. "Do you have a number where I can reach you when I get the truck back?"

"Oh. Right. Uh…" The question stung for some reason. I guess I had thought we'd be in touch before the truck was out of the tow lot. Like maybe in the morning when we awoke. But Charlie had a life here. They had a family, and it was now officially Christmas morning, and naturally they'd be busy doing other things with other people. How silly of me to presume we'd carve out time for each other.

I realized I didn't have a pen or paper to scribble down my phone number. "Here, let me put it in your phone, along with Nana's address." Since the cab's meter was still running,

I added, "And send me the receipts from today. I'll make sure we pay you back for everything." I looked at Nana's front door. She was no doubt asleep by now, but there was always the emergency money in the kitchen. "Actually, if you wait here a second, I can get some cash right now."

Charlie smiled tightly. "That would be great."

Although I had offered, I huffed as I went up the short drive to the garage and let myself inside. I knew Charlie had student loan debt, but were they really that concerned with getting money right now, tonight? After they'd held me hostage at their ex-girlfriend's house and I'd been nothing but wonderful at playing along when they'd said we were engaged? If money was such an issue, why didn't we drop Charlie off in Deerfield first? And why had Charlie bothered flirting with me and telling me they couldn't believe no one wanted to date me if this was a purely transactional relationship? I wasn't going to wear my heart on my sleeve for someone whose only commitment to me was returning luggage.

I didn't even enjoy seeing the inside of Nana's house and smelling that familiar maple syrup-jelly donut odor the place always had. I went straight to the kitchen, rooted around in the junk drawer, and found a small black lacquer box. Inside there was about five hundred dollars. I took three hundred and trotted back to the cab.

I knocked lightly on Charlie's window. When they rolled it down, I thrust the money at them. "Here. Is this enough?"

Charlie fanned out the dollar bills and frowned. "I guess, uh, okay."

Had they expected more than three hundred? I wasn't going to give it. I could pay the rest of their extortion fees when they produced my phone and purse. "Thanks for everything," I said flatly.

Charlie folded the money into their palm and looked at me. "You have a merry Christmas, Dana. I'll call you in two days."

I didn't let myself look backward as the cab pulled out of the driveway.

Back inside the house, I scribbled a note for Nana saying I had arrived and left it on the coffee maker, which I knew would be one of the first things she touched in the morning. Then I crept upstairs, blowing a kiss at her closed door, and settled into my bedroom. Since I didn't have my suitcase with my toothbrush or pajamas, I shimmied out of my clothes and nestled under the covers in my underwear. Within a matter of minutes, I had fallen into a deep sleep.

CHAPTER TWELVE

When I awoke, I could hear Nana banging around in the kitchen. We'd had several uncomfortable conversations about what Nana was capable of doing at her age and whether she should sell the house to move into a senior care facility. Nana had been insistent that her eyes were fine (they weren't), that her legs were sturdy (they weren't), and that she still had enough capacity to cook, clean, and take care of herself (she didn't). I remained skeptical, which was part of the reason I planned to surprise her with the news that I was moving home.

That morning, the sound of her making breakfast was a sweet symphony. I put my dirty clothes on and rushed down to greet her.

"Dana!" She held out her arms, and like a small child, I dove in. "I thought we'd see you yesterday."

"Oh, Nana, I cannot even begin to tell you everything that happened yesterday." I kissed her cheek before pulling away to get a cup of coffee. "Do you think you still have any of my old clothes? I lost my suitcase along the way."

"We could get you some new things."

Nana was generous to a fault, but it was Christmas, so I doubted we'd be able to go shopping. Besides that, I had to tell her, "I also lost my purse."

"You what?"

"It wasn't my fault!" I hastened to say before she chided me for being the irresponsible teenager she sometimes still thought I was. Okay, I basically was. But I insisted this time was different. "I'm the innocent victim."

Nana didn't ask me to clarify, probably because she suspected that whatever story I told would be implausible and, at the core, still my own fault. She didn't scold me either, though. "I've got extra toiletries in the hall closet, and there's some of your old college things in the basement. You can use one of my coats."

"Your coat? Are we going somewhere?"

Nana had a devilish twinkle in her eye. "We're going to Ruthie's for brunch."

It wasn't about seeing Ruthie, I knew. She wanted me to see Mitchell Wormerstein. He'd been helpful and kind on the phone the day before, and I probably owed him a thank-you in person. But I felt like an entirely different person than the one he had spoken to yesterday afternoon when he'd first called. That was a lifetime ago.

"Nana, we've talked about this." As in, we had been talking about the fact that I didn't like men for the last ten years. As in, I had been asking Nana not to try to play matchmaker for the last five. I think she needed to see me married before she lost her mental faculties or, worse, died. I could understand her anxieties and to a certain point sympathized. Who would want to think of their granddaughter alone with no family? But her attempts to matchmake were always misguided.

Case in point: Mitchell Wormerstein.

"Not a word. We're going at eleven, so you'd better be ready."

I huffed. I found a bagel to toast and spread it with some chive cream cheese. I ate with her at the kitchen table. She read the newspaper while I skimmed over all the glossy ads that came with it. I was thinking about cars and clothes and the various things we could buy if we wanted to, which made me think about Charlie and their student loan debt and their cold-hearted parents. What was Charlie's family doing right now? Were they eating breakfast happily together, bickering over old issues the way Nana and I did, full of love, or were they one of those families that ate breakfast in frosty silence? Was Charlie miserable?

I nearly wished I had their phone number, so I could check on them, when I remembered the way they'd taken the money and run.

"I had to take a cab here last night," I told Nana, "and I had to borrow some money from someone for dinner. I took cash out of the emergency box."

"We'll get some cash out on our way to Ruthie's," she declared with a nod.

Nana didn't care at all that I'd used her money. Or that the nearest ATM was in the opposite direction of Ruthie's house. What different families we had, Charlie and I, that Nana was like this. She assumed I needed it, she trusted that I'd had an emergency, and that's what the money was there for. No big deal.

"Before I forget," she said, "someone called for you." She rose slowly from her chair and shuffled across the floor. She returned with a scrap of pink paper with a number and name scrawled in her old lady cursive.

Charlie. 847-555-5499.

I took the paper from Nana with some curiosity. Charlie had said they'd call in two days. They couldn't have already gotten my purse back, since the tow lot was downtown and no doubt closed for the holiday. What did they want?

"I'll call later," I fibbed.

While we were cleaning up our breakfast dishes, I balled up the paper and threw it away. I didn't know why I did it. I only knew that my stomach fluttered anxiously at the thought of talking to Charlie. Last night those butterflies would have been exciting, full of the promise of something to come, but the way we'd parted in the driveway now meant those butterflies had kicked my fight-or-flight response into gear. Time to fly away from Charlie. We would reconnect only so that I could get my suitcase, and we'd both move on with our lives.

Before I took my shower, I found the box of clothes leftover from college that Nana had packed away. I was appreciative that she hadn't donated them and had had the foresight to imagine a day like this when I needed them, but a quick glance through the contents told me two things. One, the clothes I had worn in college were woefully out of style now. Two, even if they were fashionable, they weren't likely to fit.

After showering, I put on a pair of clean underwear—at least underwear sizes don't change that much. Then I tried the low-rise jeans Nana had ironed and creased. Way too snug. The zipper wouldn't go up, and they barely covered my ass. I opted instead for a pair of Victoria's Secret sweatpants that could accommodate my new adult size. They were pink and said so right on the butt. *Hello, this is 2007 calling. We want our pants back.*

For a shirt I managed to get into a solid black hoodie that had been my pre- and post-workout attire. At least I wasn't entirely in a matching sweatsuit. I felt horribly tacky and incredibly self-conscious, especially at the idea that Nana was going to make me go out in public in these clothes. I threw the clothes I'd been wearing in the washer, so I'd at least have them later.

Nana mostly used a senior transportation company to get around. She had quit driving at eighty, recognizing that her eyes and reflexes probably weren't good enough. That was one of the few fights over her age that I had won. I remembered being surprised when she'd agreed with me. Later Ruthie had let it slip that Nana had had a minor accident, hitting a fire hydrant but without enough force to do damage. The incident had terrified her, though, and made her think about what else she might hit with her weak eyes and slow reflexes.

The senior transportation company operated shuttles that came on demand. Though they only took passengers within a two-mile radius around Highland Park, this served Nana well enough. The only places she usually needed to go were the bank, post office, grocery store, and hair salon. For other things, she had a housekeeper named Paulina who came once a week to clean and prepare frozen meals, things like that. I had been trying to persuade her to get one of those smart speakers in the house, so she could just tell it what she wanted, and it would show up on her doorstep. Nana thought they were impersonal and said she liked having Paulina keep her company.

When I visited, we walked if the weather permitted it and if the distance wasn't far. Nana's regular physician had said it would be good to keep her active. But the sleet I had walked through the night before had frozen overnight, and the ground was now slick and dangerous. Ordinarily, I would have driven, but since I didn't have a car and neither did Nana, we opted to call a cab to get to Ruthie's.

Despite my insistence on the drive over that I was not interested in Mitchell Wormerstein, Nana kept telling me about sweet things he had done the night before. And, okay, he sounded like a pretty good guy, but the memory of him smiling over lunch with chewed up white bread stuck in his braces was relatively sharp in my mind. More importantly, Mitchell was a man, and I hadn't dated a man since sophomore year of high school—which really didn't count as dating, since all Ben Fischer and I had done was go to the movies and sit awkwardly beside each other. I was one hundred percent certain that I was not going to be interested in Mitchell Wormerstein.

Ruthie's house had no Christmas decorations on the outside, so she'd at least won that battle with Hannah. Inside, though, pine garlands and lights had been strung up in the tackiest fashion, blinking their neon colors all over the stair bannister and curlicuing over the mantle, atop which sat a wax-encrusted menorah. There was a Christmas tree, one of those cheap plastic two-foot-tall tabletop trees, which they had set on the plush white carpet in the corner of the living room. If you weren't looking for it, you wouldn't have known it was there at all. The place smelled like cinnamon and ginger, but there was klezmer music blaring from the stereo. Old people do have weaker hearing and need the volume louder than the rest of us, but this stereo was set to the levels the military might use to snuff a drug lord out of an embassy. We had entered a cultural war zone.

"Hello, my love!" Ruthie greeted me with a giant hug. I had always adored her. She was the kind of family friend who would actually remember things told to her. Once, I don't remember if it was a Thanksgiving or a Passover, but we were all gathered, and after dinner she'd sat on the arm of the sofa, playing casually with my hair while she talked to me about the ballet lessons I was taking at the time. She'd always made me feel special and loved, and I wasn't even one of her grandkids.

She put her arm around me as we made our way inside. Mitchell's dad, Larry, our token Christian for this holiest of holidays, took our coats and Nana's handbag, and Ruthie took the box of cookies Nana had brought from her favorite bakery. I held out a bottle of wine, and Larry took it as well. We were ushered into the kitchen.

There, standing in a sweater with jingle bells sewn into it, was the most handsome man I had ever seen in my life.

"Dana, you remember Mitchell," Ruthie said. "Oops, sorry, it's just Mitch now."

Mitchell Wormerstein. Mitch Stein. No wonder he'd changed his name. He needed a name to match his face. He had the finely chiseled nose of a Roman statue, the smooth tan skin of a Californian, and the physique of a swimmer. The clouds could have parted, and the sun could have shone in one careful beam onto his fine blond head while birds chirped all around him. He looked like a movie star. Like a perfect ten.

And he did absolutely nothing for me, other than stun me because of the contrast between this male model and the nosepicker I'd known in elementary school.

Do not say, "Wow," I urged myself.

"Howdy," I said, holding out my hand for a shake. "We meet at last."

"I'm glad you finally made it. We were worried about you last night."

I remembered my manners. "Yes. Thank you. You were so helpful and nice to Nana. I really appreciate it."

Mitch smiled, shooting sunbeams and rainbows out of his dimples. "It was my pleasure. Your grandma is such a great lady. I haven't seen her in a long time, but she was exactly as I remembered."

I smiled back because Nana was amazing, and it pleased me that he thought so. "So what brings you home this year?"

Mitch made a slight shushing gesture with his hand and cocked his head toward Ruthie. "We didn't think she was physically up to flying out to California this year," he said quietly. "But don't tell her I said that. She insists she's fine."

"Nana's the same way." I looked over at Ruthie, who appeared as vivacious as ever. She and Nana were a pair. They had quick wits and appeared on the outside to be relatively able-bodied, considering their age, but inside was a host of health problems they refused to let stop them. I appreciated that Mitch didn't want to miss the opportunity to spend time with Ruthie while he could.

"Golly, Mitch, how long has it been?"

"Fifteen years?" he guessed. "Maybe twenty? The last time I saw you, you still had acne."

I glared. How dare Mitchell Wormerstein suggest that I was the hot mess in junior high? "As I recall, you did too."

To his credit, he laughed. "Acne was the least of my problems. Don't you love being an adult and letting go of all those old things?"

Letting go of those old things? I'd spent the last twenty-four hours dreading this reintroduction because of all those old things. I felt frumpy and immature compared to Mitch's physical and apparently spiritual transformation. I wished my hoodie was long enough to cover the writing on my butt.

"Are you in touch with anyone else from school?" Mitch asked. "I was thinking about the Ziegler twins. Do you remember them?"

The Ziegler twins were a pair of fraternal twins who had terrorized our junior high teachers. Marta liked to feign illnesses, rallying the sympathies of female classmates and ensuring she didn't have to attend classes because she'd be sent to the nurse. I couldn't recall what her grades were, but looking back, I suspected she was a terrible student and her increasingly outlandish illnesses were a theatrical way of covering up her academic flaws.

Daniel was equally gregarious, though a more serious student. His claim to fame was playing practical jokes on teachers. He'd once stolen Mrs. Coleman's Kaopectate from her desk drawer—when it was forbidden to even go near a teacher's desk—and he'd then tried to sell it back to her when she went looking for it later. He'd said it was a funny coincidence that he just happened to have a bottle, which he'd gladly share for twenty bucks. Mrs. Coleman had not been amused, but everyone else in class had. All the boys wanted to be him. I had had a giant crush on him. I hadn't thought about him in years, but now that Mitch had mentioned the name, I remembered that I'd once summoned the courage to talk to Daniel during a junior high dance. A slow song had come on, and Mitch had asked me to dance with him, interrupting my conversation with Daniel and what I thought at the time was the beginning of my first ever date. Instead, I'd spent three minutes swaying from one foot to the other with my arms looped around Mitchell Wormerstein's neck, our bodies a good yard apart.

"Do you remember the junior high dances?" I asked. *Do you remember how you ruined my chances with one of the Ziegler twins, and now I turned out gay?*

"Yeah." Mitch smiled easily. Clearly his memories were better than my own. "I remember once asking you to dance when I saw you chasing Daniel Ziegler around the dance floor like a lost puppy. I felt so sorry for you."

That was definitely not how things had gone! Mitch's memory from our twelfth year of life was completely skewed. I had been reasonably popular.

Or had I just always followed the popular crowd like a dorky outsider trying to blend in? What if it wasn't Mitchell

Wormerstein at all who was the outcast? What if it had been me?

"Do you mean to tell me you only danced with me because you took pity on me?"

"Well, Dana, I thought we nerds had to stick together."

That confirmed it. I'd spent the last two days dreading a reunion with Mitchell Wormerstein, dweeb extraordinaire on whom I, Dana Gottfried, hierarchy rank medium, cool factor not perfect but definitely above his, had taken pity. And in Mitchell's reality, *I* had been the dweeb, and I had been the recipient of *his* pity.

"Oh geez, Mitch, we were both social outcasts, weren't we?"

"But look at us now," he said proudly. "Look how far we've come."

He was wearing a sweater with jingle bells sewn into it, and I looked like I was auditioning for a drill team. I had no car, no job, no meaningful friendships, and no love life. How far indeed.

Admittedly, it took a while for me to accept Mitch's version of our shared past and to stop feeling so stung that my perception of myself as a child had been so removed from reality. As we stood over a bowl of hot artichoke dip and crackers, little bits of grade school and junior high came back to me. I remembered that my crush on Daniel had been calculated. I had thought he was attractive, but I had also hoped that if I married him, I could get closer to Marta. Now, with my revisionist queer lens, I wondered if it was because I was actually attracted to her all along. I remembered that she never gave me the time of day. She had a wide circle of fawning admirers from our class, but I'd always stood apart from them, confused about how to behave in her presence and never quite doing or saying the right things to make them like me.

Face it, Dana. You were as big a loser as Mitchell Wormerstein. A lesbian who didn't yet know she was one, struggling to reconcile her unconscious, burgeoning feelings with her basic need for the intimacy of female friendships. The other students must have thought I was so weird.

This revelation would need a lot more time to process, but in that moment it made it a lot easier to accept the company of Mitch Stein. I found it was enjoyable to talk to him. Eventually we were all instructed to sit around the dining table, and the conversation moved to general catching up among friends and family. It was good to see Ruthie, Lila, and even Hannah, who asked me what Santa Claus had brought me that morning.

"Mom!" Mitch sounded embarrassed. "He didn't bring her anything."

"Uh-oh, were you naughty?" Hannah teased me.

I looked at Nana and then at Mitch. Somewhere in her marriage to Larry, Hannah had gone bananas. "I guess I was," I said gamely. "Really, really naughty." I winked at the table for good measure, playing into the possible double meaning. Everyone just looked blankly back at me.

Charlie would have laughed.

We ate about a third of the mountains of food Ruthie and Lila had prepared, and then Hannah and I spent a half hour cleaning the kitchen and putting the leftovers away.

While we were working, the others decided we should go to a movie. Nana needed to take her pills if she was going to be out all afternoon, so we piled into two cars and drove the short distance to our house. And then the curse of the big group happened. Everyone had a different idea about where to go and which movie to see, and tribalism quickly broke out. Mitch and I escaped the squabbling older generation by taking a bottle of red zinfandel into the living room.

Despite my initial trepidation, he was all right, and we were laughing as we reminisced. As it turned out, I had largely misremembered his dorkiest moments, and he'd definitely blossomed into someone with more panache. At the same time, he'd reminded me of a few things I had conveniently forgotten. In addition to my acne, there was the time I accidentally peed in temple because I was too scared to ask where the bathroom was. And the reason why I'd spent so many indoor recesses playing with him—because I, too, had had no one else to play with. We were laughing over our seventh grade math teacher's tendency to smoke in the janitor's closet right before class when the doorbell rang.

"Are you expecting company?" he asked.

"I don't think so. Nana didn't tell me we had any guests coming."

Ruthie hurried past us, telling us not to bother getting up, that she'd get it, in the manner of a highly efficient woman used to doing everything, even when it wasn't her house.

A moment later, she walked into the room with Charlie. Their hair was freshly combed back with gel, and their cheeks were pink from the cold. They were wearing a black velvet blazer, a tuxedo shirt, and glittery silver loafers. They looked like they'd scrubbed off the pigs and were ready to sip a martini at an exclusive nightclub.

I gaped. I wanted.

From his place on the couch next to me, Mitch asked, "Dana, who's this?"

I watched as Charlie turned from nervous and hopeful to embarrassed and defeated. Their smile never faltered, and I doubted Ruthie and Mitch picked up on the change. But I saw it. I felt it in the air.

"This is Charlie," I said, as if that explained everything. "Um, Charlie, this is—this is…"

"I'm Mitch," he supplied, setting down his wine. He got to his feet to shake Charlie's hand.

"I've obviously made a big mistake," they mumbled. "I'm sorry to have interrupted your Christmas." They turned and raced out of the room.

I ran after them, calling their name. They let me catch them when they got to the front door.

"Charlie, what are you doing here?"

"I thought…I guess I just thought…I didn't want to let things go the way they were," they admitted, "but I didn't realize. I feel so stupid." To my surprise, their eyes were glassy with tears. "You didn't say you were bi or queer. You said you were a lesbian. When you were calling him last night, it didn't occur to me that you might be together."

I looked back over my shoulder to see Mitch coming toward us with a look of concern on his face. Bad timing. I hurriedly turned back to Charlie. "No, you don't understand. It's not like that."

"Dana," Mitch asked, "are you—is this…?" He gestured between him and me.

My hands came up to cover my face. I didn't know how to explain quickly enough to stop everything from becoming a mess, and I didn't understand why Charlie had come and how they had even found the house. I knew Charlie thought Mitch and I were together, and now it sounded as if Mitch thought I was with Charlie but coming on to him. Maybe I had liked the attention, but I wasn't interested in him. I gave up men a long time ago, and I could appreciate that he was attractive, but I didn't want him. At all. And I definitely didn't want him to be the reason Charlie was now trying to run away.

"I should go," Charlie said.

"No, you stay," Mitch told them. "I should give you some privacy."

"Mitch, wait," I started, and that was all it took for Charlie to bolt. With futility, I called after them and ran down the front steps, but they jumped into a black SUV that had plastic reindeer antlers sticking out of the front windows and sped away.

Mitch came down the stairs after me. "Was that your... boyfriend?"

"No," I nearly cried. "We just met last night, but I think they think you and I are dating."

Mitch was taken aback. "Dana, that's what I was trying to say. I hope I didn't give you the wrong idea. I've really enjoyed catching up with you, and I'm really flattered by your interest in me, but I'm already seeing someone."

"What?"

"He's in Phoenix with his family. We aren't exactly at the 'spend the holidays with each other's family' stage yet, but..." He grinned that TV game show host smile again. "I think we could be eventually."

"That's great, Mitch," I said distractedly. I was too busy wondering where Charlie had gone and why they had rushed off so quickly to care much about Mitchell Wormerstein's dating life. Why had Charlie even come over this morning? If I had wanted to talk, I would have called them back. But, damn, they had looked fine. What was that all about? Why were they so dressed up? Had Mitch just said "he"?

"Wait a second. Are you telling me you have a *boyfriend*?"

"Yeah." He gave me a soul-searching look. "I hope that's not a problem. I know our grandmothers want to play matchmaker, and I thought you were a little interested, but I wasn't sure how to tell you because I didn't want to hurt your feelings. If you're dating that person who just left—"

"You're gay?" I repeated. *Hello, my name is Dana, and I need to hear things multiple times to believe them.*

"Yes."

"You're gay?" The third time it registered. "But so am I."

"You are?"

"Yes." I started laughing. Hard. Maybe a little too hard. The absurdity of the last day overwhelmed me, and it finally came out in full-bellied, side-splitting guffaws. Nothing had worked out the way it was supposed to, for any of us. Nana and Ruthie weren't going to get their marriage of unity between Mitch and me, for a lot more reasons than they realized. Mitch had clearly liked the idea of me flirting with him, though he didn't want to reciprocate. What an ego, I thought, and how terrible that I had to crush it. Meanwhile, I just wanted...

What did I want?

I looked down the street in the direction Charlie had gone. The way they had taken the money last night and left, I had assumed they were done with me. Once they got rid of all my junk in their car, anyway. But they had shown up here, unexpectedly. Why? How? Whose car was that? Why were they dressed so nicely? They looked so good cleaned up. Not that I hadn't found Charlie attractive in jeans and a raggedy canvas coat the day before, but this polished version made my heart quicken. Had they dressed up just to see me? There was no mistaking that they were disappointed to believe Mitch and I were together. Did that mean they didn't want to see me with someone else? Because they were interested in me?

I wanted that to be the case, I realized. I thought of how they'd pulled up beside me on the side of the road what seemed like a lifetime ago and of how they'd come back to the diner after leaving me there. How they hadn't left the train station when we both thought I was once again safely on my way but instead waited to make sure. When I had missed the train, Charlie had been there with a donut and a shoulder to cry on. In the last twenty-four hours, Charlie had proven to be the most dependable person in my life.

I didn't care if they had lied to Caroline about us getting engaged to save face. I didn't care about the student loan payments or the pigs or the pronouns. No, that wasn't right. I did care. I loved it. All of it. I loved the person it meant Charlie was. Charlie was weird and wonderful and had shown nothing but kindness to me and everyone we'd met on our journey. Charlie didn't look like Mitch. Charlie's beauty came from the inside, radiating outward, and their eyes were open windows to their deep, tranquil soul. The fluid way Charlie moved their body was purely erotic, and I couldn't forget the electricity I'd felt when they allowed me to touch them during our pretend engagement.

They had borrowed a car with reindeer antlers to see me, and I hadn't even gotten to hear what they wanted to say.

It didn't matter as much as what I needed to say to them.

"Mitch, I need a car and a phone," I announced with newfound purpose. Nothing in my chaotic life had ever been as clear to me as what I had to do in that moment. "I have to get to Deerfield."

Chapter Thirteen

I was in such a hurry that it didn't even occur to me to stop and look for the balled up paper with Charlie's number in the trash can. I didn't give myself a chance to look up an address before tearing out of the driveway. I kept Mitch's phone braced against the steering wheel with one hand while I yanked the car around turns with the other. Charlie had thankfully told me their last name—Barlow—so I tried desperately to search for that name online. Like most people our age, Charlie was easily found on social media, but their phone number and address were not listed in the white pages.

At a stoplight, I remembered that Charlie and Mitch had messaged each other through Facebook. I looked to see if Mitch had the app on his phone. Success! I sent a frantic message back to Charlie, reading, "It's me! Where do you live and what is your phone number?"

I couldn't afford to wait for Charlie to read it.

I tried to look for their family instead. There were two listings for Barlows in Deerfield, Illinois. One had an old-fashioned landline attached to their listing, so I immediately called it. No one answered. I looked at the other entry. The address wasn't too far off Deerfield Road, one of the main throughways in the little suburb. I was pretty sure I knew how to get there, but I took a second to pull up a map to be sure. I might have had to swerve to avoid hitting a light pole, and I swore and yanked the steering wheel back. I needed to be more careful. Hitting a light pole would slow me down from my mission. Hitting another car would mean ruining someone else's life the way the driver of the car that fateful night had ruined my parents' and mine. No way did I want that.

I routed the phone GPS through the car stereo speakers. It told me I'd be at the other Barlow house in nine minutes.

I really, really hoped Charlie had gone back to their parents' house. If they hadn't, this would be a futile quest.

Nine minutes later, I arrived at a split-level house with white siding and an empty driveway. The front walk had been neatly shoveled and salted, and there were rows of dangling icicle lights hanging off the roof of the front porch. I rang the bell once, holding my breath, but nothing happened. I rang it again and waited. And waited. The adrenaline I'd felt when I'd jumped in Ruthie's Lexus was fading as part of me began to accept that this chase wasn't going to end the way I wanted.

Since no one was home, there was no way for me to confirm I was even at the right house. I rang the doorbell once more, to be sure, and knocked in case the bell didn't work. I looked over my shoulder to see if anyone was moving around the block. Would they think I was nuts for banging on the Barlows' door? Would they be able to tell me where the Barlows were? It didn't matter. There were cars up and down the street, signs of family gatherings, but everyone was settled inside. The street was bare of people.

After another interminable minute, I accepted that no one was home and got back in the car.

What was I supposed to do? Was it a cosmic sign that I should give up? I didn't like that possibility. I didn't want to give up. I wanted to tell Charlie how I felt, and I believed the universe was rooting for us to find each other. I decided to retrace my steps a few blocks to a strip mall with a coffee shop, where I figured I could regroup and give the internet search my full attention.

On the short drive, I thought through my options. I could search for Caroline and Clint and ask them to intervene. Caroline wouldn't do it, but Clint might. Charlie had said he was "good people." And he had been nice enough to call a cab for me. I could call Nana and have someone dig through the trash for the piece of paper with Charlie's number that I'd thrown out that morning. I shuddered to think what kind of food waste was now on top of it, but if it meant a chance to get a hold of Charlie directly, I'd go through the trash myself. I wasn't sure how well Nana and Ruthie would take the request, though.

Deerfield, Illinois, was not a big enough place for me to lose Charlie, but I had no guarantee that Charlie had gone back to Deerfield. They could have been anywhere in the greater Chicago area. Caroline's condo. Some other friend's house. A favorite bar. Anywhere. And if that were the case, I'd never find them without phone contact.

As I pulled into the parking lot of the café, I checked Mitch's Facebook app optimistically. No new messages.

I folded my arms on the gray leather steering wheel and buried my head in them. I chastised myself for being such an idiot that I didn't recognize how much I wanted Charlie until they were gone. I probably wouldn't see them again until they got the truck out of the city impound lot, and then it would be a five-minute exchange with all the pleasantry of an airline delivering a lost bag. *Here's your suitcase, Dana. Nice meeting you. Bye.*

I didn't want that. I wanted to kiss Charlie's plush mouth. I wanted to hold Charlie's hand. I wanted to feel our bodies against each other the way they had been at Caroline's house. I wanted to see what was inside the cabin in the woods.

"Come on, kiddo," I said aloud. "At least go inside to think."

I lifted my head from the steering wheel and unbuckled my seat belt. I got out of the car and shut the door. I took two steps toward the coffee shop door and stopped. A few spaces away from where I'd parked was a black SUV with reindeer antlers affixed to the windows.

I knew instantly that I was about to see Charlie and that I was going to make this right. I could feel Charlie's cosmic presence. A wave of confidence swept over me. Never once in my thirty-two years of existence had I ever rushed after someone to tell them how I felt about them. Until today.

I ran inside.

It took me a second to spot them, Charlie and Clint seated in purple velveteen chairs in front of a gas fireplace.

They saw me.

"Dana, what are you doing here?" Charlie passed their coffee cup to Clint and got to their feet. "How did you find me?"

I was beaming. "I'm doing the same thing you were doing at Nana's, and I found you the same way you found me."

Charlie didn't smile back. "Dana, it's okay. I obviously misread everything that happened between us, and that's fine. I thought you were only into women, and I'm kicking myself that I hadn't realized about you and Mitch sooner. The way you were talking about him yesterday, I should have known. I'm just embarrassed I made such a scene in front of your family."

"There's nothing going on between me and Mitch!" I nearly screamed. The next words came out in a frantic rush, as if taking too long to explain might risk losing Charlie again. "We were talking about old memories from grade school, and he made me realize I used to be a loser, too, and that made me really excited because you don't see me as a loser, and Mitch is gay and has a boyfriend in Phoenix, and when I look at him, I don't feel anything." I took a deep breath and steadied myself for the big moment. "Because my feelings are for you."

Charlie's brown eyes softened. "That's crazy," they said, but their words were betrayed by their actions as their hands reached for my hips. "We just met."

"Charlie, no one has ever made me feel the way you do. I'm falling for you. Tell me you don't feel it back."

The hands on my hips squeezed. I could feel the pressure even beneath Nana's green wool coat. "I feel it, too," Charlie said softly.

"Is it okay that we're doing this in front of Clint?" Charlie nodded again, and I gathered the courage to ask, "Can I kiss you?"

Charlie grinned. "Darlin', I have wanted to kiss you since I first saw you on the side of the road."

My breath caught, and my knees threatened to give out from under me. I was falling into the depths of Charlie's eyes, but I knew they'd catch me. I wanted to kiss them more than I had ever wanted anything.

Charlie leaned forward, tilting their head to the right, and their silken pillows of lips found mine. I wanted to open my mouth and taste them, but I was aware that we were in public and Clint was watching us.

When we parted, Charlie pressed their forehead to mine. Their hand found mine and laced our fingers together. Real hand-holding. Not like the "make sure we don't get separated" hand-holding from the night before. This was romance.

My whole body warmed, and it wasn't because of the fireplace.

"Clint," Charlie called, "you remember my girlfriend, Dana?"

"I thought she was your fiancée," Clint reminded us.

We laughed, and I settled on a chair beside them. Charlie never let go of my hand.

"It's good to see you again, Miss Thang," Clint greeted me. "I hope you had a good night. I'd ask if Santa Claus was good to you, but…fuck that corporate capitalist made-up bullshit to sell greeting cards and presents and deny the existence of the Jews, am I right?"

I loved Clint. "What are you doing up here?" I asked him. "Do you live on the North Shore?"

Clint made a puzzled face. "You were at my house last night."

I was? Granted, my adventure with Charlie had taken me to lots of unexpected places the night before, but the only house we had been at was…

"You live with Caroline?"

He scoffed. "She had to move in with me after Esperanza dumped her. You think she could afford her own condo? Puh-lease."

My brain could not process what I was hearing.

"That's your house? Not Caroline's?" I looked to Charlie for confirmation. Charlie nodded, a quizzical look on their face. Had they not understood how awful it had been to think we were going to Caroline's house to pretend Caroline and Charlie were still a couple? How awful it had been to think about Caroline and Charlie ever being together? How confused I had been that Charlie had even called Caroline in the first place? "So that's *your* condo?" I repeated for good measure.

"Yes, Dane," Charlie said emphatically.

The swanky condo belonged to Clint. I remembered Charlie telling me Caroline had moved in with her new girlfriend and Caroline tersely telling us it hadn't worked out. If they'd moved in together, and she'd given up her place, Caroline must have been homeless. So she'd moved in with her brother, but her hoity-toity attitude would naturally make her act as if she owned the place.

And if it were Clint's house and Clint's party, it made a little more sense why Charlie had wanted to go. They had been friends for a long time. Charlie wasn't trying to get back together with Caroline. Charlie was trying to get back together with their bestie.

"Okay," I said, "so you live in Oak Park in a very nice condo—which, by the way, thank you for having me over last night, it was a very nice party, you have excellent taste in champagne—but why are you in Deerfield on Christmas Day? Is your family up here, too?"

"He's rescuing me," Charlie admitted. "I told him I planned to find you, and he came in case it didn't go well."

"Since I couldn't rescue you both last night," Clint added.

Last night? I thought back on the night. We had asked Clint to drive me home after the party, but he'd called a cab instead. That wasn't a failure to rescue.

The car accident. The car getting towed. Had Charlie called Clint? Had Caroline arrived as his proxy? I'd spent the night pissy and uncomfortable that Charlie was still obsessed with Caroline, but maybe I'd been wrong about the entire situation.

"Oh my gosh, Clint, that is really, really sweet of you!" It hadn't sunk in that we weren't talking about an abstract situation here. Charlie was nervous to find *me*. They had been talking about *me*.

"I was actually at my parents' house, too," he admitted. "They live in Northbrook."

Northbrook was another adjacent suburb. Also very populated with Jewish people. Also very affluent. Maybe Charlie's world and mine weren't so different.

"It looks like Charlie doesn't need much rescuing," Clint observed with a benevolent smile. Clearly, somewhere between our conversation in the bathroom the night before and now, he'd given the idea of Charlie and me his stamp of approval.

I turned to Charlie. "Speaking of parents, how did it go?"

"They're actually on their way here."

"Oh!" I tried to imagine a family of homophobes walking into a coffee shop to find their genderqueer child holding hands with a female stranger. That wasn't going to make Charlie's life any easier. I dropped their hand. "Okay, let me get out of here then, and we can meet up later? If you want? Or maybe you're busy with family stuff all day?"

"I would like you to meet them."

"But I thought…"

My murmured confusion didn't get fully expressed. Clint announced he needed a refill, and a moment later a flock of people pushed through the front door as a jazzy rendition of "Jingle Bells" with saxophone started playing. I was intimidated at the sheer size of the Barlow family compared to my own. Where my family was just Nana and I, two people identical in size but separated in age by fifty years, the Barlows were a crowd of different heights and weights and ages. They found Charlie and surrounded us, Viking invaders disrupting our tranquil coffee shop romance. Charlie introduced them clockwise: their mother, Lydia; father, Preston; brother Pete; brother Joe; sister-in-law, Carly; aunt Horty—*Horty?* really?— and their teenage cousin, Arabella. They all greeted me politely, but the story Charlie had told me the night before about coming out and being rejected by them was burning on my mind.

"Everyone, this is Dana." I heard something in Charlie's voice that took me a moment to identify. Pride. Charlie was proud to introduce me to them.

"Merry Christmas, Dana," Charlie's father said cheerily. With his potbelly and retro glasses, he was hardly the evil patriarch I'd imagined.

"She's Jewish, Dad," Charlie told him. Preston looked embarrassed at his mistake.

"I had a really good Hanukkah this year," I assured him.

Charlie explained, "We were all meeting up before going to a movie. It's kind of our annual tradition. Do you want to hang out with us a little before we go?"

"Dana?" Charlie's mom interrupted. She was wringing her hands but sounded sweet enough. "Would you like to come to the movie with us?"

I looked at the Barlows, overwhelmed at this very public reception and confused by their mirth and warmth. I hadn't pictured my big, romantic declaration to Charlie to also be my first time meeting their parents.

"Let's not pressure her," Charlie said. "She might have stuff to do with her own family."

Still in a fog, I heard myself say I'd join them for a few minutes for coffee and allowed myself to be led to the counter to order. In keeping with the spirit of the day, I got a peppermint mocha. Charlie offered to pay for it, but since I now had Nana's spare debit card, I insisted on paying for myself. I didn't want money to be a source of tension between us, especially not after the way we'd said good-bye the night before.

Charlie intuited my concerns. "I'm not offering to pay because your purse is in my truck, and I feel sorry for you. I'm not offering a loan. I'm offering to buy you a cup of coffee the way I would offer to buy you dinner if we went out."

How could I say no to that?

"Okay, but you should still buy me dinner."

"I'll buy you a lot of dinners," Charlie pledged, pushing their debit card into the card reader. I peeked and saw they added a fifteen percent tip. Classy.

Clint's drink came up, and he took it back to where the Barlows were sitting. I watched him sit down with them, old chums catching up, carefree, and wondered how the Barlows felt about Clint's flamboyant personality. The store music channel began playing a punk rock version of "Santa Baby." The music was as confusing as the situation.

"I don't get it, Charlie," I had to say. "I thought you didn't get along with them. I thought they hated that you're queer." I gestured to Clint and his best friends, Lydia and Preston Suburbia. "He's not exactly straight-passing. And what about us? Your mom invited me to a movie! Does she know we're dating?" I said it without thinking, and as soon as it was out of my mouth, I backpedaled in humiliation. "Uh, I mean, are we dating? I mean…We haven't had a *date*, but…I just mean…" In my haste, I blurted the dumbest thing possible. "We don't have to define this."

Dana, you complete idiot. Talk about misrepresenting myself and my desires. I wanted "this" defined. I needed it defined. I was not the kind of person who could ever survive in a non-defined relationship. Which wouldn't even be a relationship because that would be defining it. How people coupled without commitment or labels was way, way beyond my sensibility. If that made me a bad lesbian who was enslaved to the hetero-monogamy matrix, so be it. I didn't want to make a political statement. I just wanted someone to be proud to call me theirs.

Charlie was holding my hand, and they brought it now to their lips and kissed my knuckles. I blushed at the chivalry. "Maybe we don't have to define it, but we should. When we're ready."

Logically, I knew the punk styling of "Santa Baby" was playing in the background, but I heard Whitney Houston belting out the final chorus to "I Will Always Love You." I wasn't sure how I remained upright and didn't faint from the thrill of Charlie wanting to define a relationship with me.

"Are you going to be okay?"

I let Whitney draw out her last "youuuuuuuuu" before I nodded and told Charlie that, yes, I was more than okay. "You make me happy."

"Me too. I want to kiss you again." Charlie glanced at their family and cleared their throat. "So, listen, Dane, I have some news."

"Okay…" I guessed I wasn't getting that kiss.

"You know how I told you my parents rejected me, and I didn't really want to come here?"

Charlie might have left Indiana a day early because they had the hots for me, but that wasn't the only reason. Charlie clearly had a lot of unresolved stuff with their family. That had been clear in the truck when they'd refused to talk much about them. And later in the cab, when they'd explained why they kept Caroline around. Part of Charlie might have hated their parents for being ignorant transphobes, but part of them also desperately wanted their parents' love and approval. And why wouldn't they? If my parents were still alive, I'd put up with just about anything they did or said to be around them. We could always work on growing and changing. We couldn't exactly work on them being dead.

"Yeah, but at the same time, you did really want to come. You just wanted them to change their attitudes," I added.

Charlie smirked. "Okay, you're a little too insightful, and you're spoiling my punchline."

"I'm sorry. Tell me."

"Last night, after the cab dropped me off, my parents were waiting up for me. We had a big talk. They told me they realize how stupid they've been and how wrong they were. And that they're proud of me for living my truth."

Their voice hitched a little, and I wondered how long it had been since they'd heard that from their parents—or if they ever had. My own parents had lavished me with love and praise. They were strict with rules, but even when I was in trouble, I never doubted they loved me and were proud of me.

"Oh, Charlie, I'm so happy for you! Did they say why now?"

"They've been going to a lot of counseling." There was a pause. "I wasn't exactly truthful with you about my trip here."

"Oh?"

"I told my parents this would be the last time I would come to see them until they could understand and support me. I didn't mean it as an empty threat," Charlie explained. I wouldn't have expected them to have made idle threats. They seemed like the type who followed through on their word, and I could imagine saying something like that to their parents must have been difficult. "They said the more they tried to picture our family without me, the worse it seemed, so they knew there had to be a change. And that the change wasn't my responsibility. It was theirs."

My face must have made one giant "O" of surprise. "Charlie, that is amazing! How do you feel?"

"Really lucky. I feel like there is some justice in the world." They poked me. "Guess what else? They reinstated my trust fund."

"You have a trust fund?"

Charlie nodded. "I do now. Enough to cover my student loan payments."

I didn't hear the barista call my drink. Charlie did, and they took it and handed it to me gallantly. My head was still spinning. "This is a lot to take in."

That cocky attitude that had first attracted me reemerged. "You mean because you thought you were falling for a poor farmer?"

I took a well-timed sip of my drink. It was all whipped cream.

"Does that change anything for you?" Charlie asked.

"No," I said, and I meant it. I thought I meant it, at least. The idea of Charlie rich was incongruous with the picture they'd created in the last day of themselves as a farmer in rural Indiana, driving a rusty old truck and tending to pigs that I still hadn't seen any proof of. Plus, if Charlie was now going to be flush with cash, we were going to be on unequal footing. I could tell from the way Charlie announced their financial woes were over that they suspected me of being a brat who would find them more attractive with money, but that was because Charlie assumed I had money, too. I was broke. And unemployed.

I probably needed to tell Charlie that as soon as possible.

Their mother came over to us. Standing beside Charlie, I could see the family resemblance. She was much more heavyset, but they were about the same height and had the same eyes.

"I'm sorry to interrupt you girls—uh, people." She cringed at her mistake. "But if we're still going to that movie, we should get going." She looked at Charlie hopefully. "Maybe you'd prefer to skip it, under the circumstances?"

I was the circumstances.

"Of course," she continued, "you're more than welcome to come with us, Dana. Our treat."

Charlie's mom was not doing a good job at being stoic. It was clear she did not want to leave her child, now that they had found a way to reconnect. She wanted Charlie to come to the movie, and although her invitation to me was kind, I could tell she'd only offered as a way of pleasing Charlie. I was willing to bet that she'd prefer if I weren't around to distract Charlie from family time.

I was torn. I couldn't fathom a worse way to try to get to know people than to sit in the dark silently with them for two hours, and going to the movies with people I didn't know very well always made me stress out over how much popcorn I ate. But I didn't want to leave Charlie's side now that I had them, especially if we only had a little time together before we both headed to our separate, distant homes.

I also didn't want to be the reason Charlie missed a chance to be with their family, and I suspected Charlie wouldn't go if I said I wasn't. That would be a mistake on Charlie's part. Because their parents were alive, they didn't know how precious every missed opportunity to spend time with them was. I had spent ten Hanukkahs without my parents. Ten years of coming to Highland Park between Christmas and New Year's without my mother and father, ten birthdays without cards or gifts or phone calls from them, ten summers without family vacations. There was nothing—not a new love, not a broken down car, not even other people in a car accident—that I wouldn't ignore to spend one more minute with them.

"I stole a phone and a car to get here," I said gently, not thinking about how that might sound to Lydia. "I should get back, and we can hook up later?"

"We can hook up later" was an unfortunate choice of phrase to use in front of someone's mother. My own had lived long enough to experience the awkward years of high school and college dating. When I told my dad my dorm was co-ed, he'd wanted to stop payment on my tuition check and bring me home. Within a matter of months, it was the girls, not the boys, that he should have worried about.

"Are you sure?" Charlie asked.

"Yes." In case it wasn't registering to them, I added, "I don't have a mom, and yours is right here, and she is trying to make things right with you. If not for her sake, then you owe it to yourself to try. I would kill for that chance."

Charlie's eyes were moist with tears as they nodded. Lydia took my hand and gave it a motherly squeeze. "I hope we get to know you better, Dana." Her voice cracked on my name.

I saw the Barlows out to the parking lot, where we waved and parted company. Charlie walked me to Ruthie's gold Lexus.

"Nice ride," they said. The car was roughly the size of a boat and had been freshly washed clean of any winter salt.

That unfortunately meant it also glimmered garishly in the winter sun.

"My grandma's friend's. Mitchell Wormerstein's grandma."

"Say hi to old Mitch for me."

"I will." I opened the door and lingered before getting in. I bit my lip. "I'll see you later tonight?"

Charlie peered over the roof of the car to check on the SUV and the family. Then they ducked back, a little out of sight of the curious Barlow eyes. "I hope I see *a lot* of you tonight."

I gasped, but they captured my mouth in a kiss before I could react. I felt every nerve in my body electrify. My palms clenched with a need to be thrown to the ground and ravished. I wanted Charlie more than I had ever wanted anyone in my life.

CHAPTER FOURTEEN

By the time I got back to Nana's house, the party had broken up. Ruthie and the Wormersteins had gone home with instructions that we were to keep Ruthie's car until the next day. Nana told me they'd left because Mitchell was headed out on an early flight the next morning. I pretended not to hear the disappointment in her voice, and I gave her the courtesy of not telling her that he was heading home to a new love interest of his own. The fact that Mitchell Wormerstein—Mitch Stein—was gay would be a surprise for another day, although I couldn't understand why Ruthie had never mentioned it to Nana. Likely she was in the same denial. Neither was homophobic. They just really believed that one day their kids would get together.

Since it was already evening, I decided to take advantage of the fact that Nana and I had a car by taking Nana out for Chinese like a good Jewish family. It wasn't something we did every year, but we had done it a few times. Nana had only begun to like Chinese food fairly recently, and I was slowly introducing her to other Americanized versions of world cuisines. She'd found Thai food too spicy, which was my fault for ordering a spice level two instead of one when the server asked for our preference. Weirdly, she found Indian food not spicy enough, which was probably the result of me worrying about spice levels after the Thai food. I wanted to introduce her to sushi, but Nana had put her foot down to that.

In Highland Park and the surrounding suburbs, there were a lot of Chinese and pan-Asian restaurants open on Christmas. They ranged from mom-and-pop storefront takeout places with one or two tables to elaborate pagodas with white linen tablecloths and rice paper lanterns. The one thing they all had in common was that they were hopping on Christmas, not just from the number of Jewish families avoiding a traditional meal at home but from all the other people who got sick of eating turkey and the hours of cooking and cleaning. Eating Chinese on Christmas had become more popular throughout my life, and I knew that Nana and I would have a long wait wherever we went.

It would have made more sense to stay home or place a takeout order, but I wanted to be sitting down in public when I told her about Charlie and my job. Maybe I thought doing it in public would eliminate any possibility of shouting. Not that Nana ever shouted. It wasn't her style. But if pressed to defend my life choices, I might.

I was looking forward to my rendezvous with Charlie at nine, our first chance to be together as a couple, but now that the thrill of the moment had settled, I was starting to get nervous. First, there was the fact that I hadn't told Charlie I had quit the art museum and was planning to move out of Cleveland. This could be a game-changer in terms of any relationship we expected to have together. Cleveland was much closer to Charlie's house than Chicago was. Plus, I only really had enough money to cover my move. By January, I'd be flat broke and desperate if I didn't find employment fast. To someone who had just come into a trust fund, that was probably a major turn-off.

Then there was the sex stuff. Charlie made my body pulse when they kissed me, but I had been a self-described lesbian for my entire adult life. Charlie was not a woman. Neither was Charlie a man. I'd never had sex with a man, but at least I knew the fundamentals of how to do it from television. I had no idea how to be with someone who identified as genderqueer. Were there parts of Charlie's body they wouldn't want me to touch? Who was going to be the top? The penetrator? The active partner? Whatever the politically correct vocabulary was these days, I didn't know who was going to do what, and that made me nervous—even though I was horny from way too many months alone and desperate to be with someone I thought I could fall in love with. I wanted hot passion, tangled sheets, and sweaty bodies. I also wanted tender cuddling, spooning while we slept, and the warm feeling of trust.

But how could Charlie trust me when I had spent two days being less than honest?

Because of all these nerves, I was distracted over dinner with Nana. We went to the linen tablecloth kind of restaurant, and after a half hour of standing like sardines in the entryway, we were finally seated. We ordered three entrees, crab rangoon, and eggrolls, way more food than we could eat, especially since Nana ate like a bird. The restaurant was deafeningly loud, of course, jam-packed with families. Our table was observably less festive and chatty. Nana wasn't prodding me, thankfully, but it was obvious something was on my mind. After several long minutes of silence, I mustered the courage to speak.

"Nana, do you think I've been happy with my job at the museum?"

She thought for a moment before speaking. "There are things you like and seem satisfied with, but I'm not sure it's your dream job. I don't think it gives you the fulfillment I had hoped."

"Why haven't you ever said anything before?"

"I didn't think it was my place. You have to find out for yourself what you want."

"And what about Cleveland? Do you think I'm happy there?"

She had visited once. We'd gone to dinner and the theater and spent time at Edgewater Park, which was situated on a bluff overlooking Lake Erie. The winds came rushing off the lake, and it was a popular spot for gliders. For picnicking, it was less than ideal, but on a clear day the view was incredible. Nana's visit had been nice enough, but I didn't think Nana had gotten many insights into my life. I rarely spent time picnicking on Lake Erie. Mostly I ate microwaveable meals while watching TLC.

"I'm eighty-five," Nana reminded me. "I think I've earned the right to speak candidly."

"Okay…but you just said you didn't think it was your place to speak up."

She silenced me with a sharp look. Apparently, when she decided it was her time to talk, I was supposed to shut up and listen.

"Sometimes I think about how lonely you are, and it worries me. I think about dying and you're still alone. I think about how hard you are trying to make a life for yourself in Cleveland, and it's not working. You're not happy. You're chasing something that's not right for you. I want to see you happy."

The half-eaten eggroll I'd been working on dropped to the table as I burst into tears. "Nana," I blubbered, "I don't think I've been happy at all! I screwed up everything with my job because I'm not good at that kind of work. Schmoozing and keeping my mouth shut. And then I thought I was going to get fired, so I quit, and then on the way here, my car broke down, and I couldn't even afford to get it fixed, but the guy—Sam, the mechanic—he said it's not fixable, and that's when I met Charlie."

"Who's Charlie? The one that called the house?"

I wiped my tears away, my face softening to a blissful smile. "Nana, Charlie's the most wonderful person in the world. Do you know Charlie is trying to protect pigs from unethical farming? Or something like that anyway. And when there was the car accident, Charlie rushed in to help, and I thought Charlie was trying to get back together with Caroline, but it was just because of Clint, and—"

"Slow down, Dana."

I took a breath and steadied myself, one hand on the table for support. I looked Nana in the eye. "I told you a long time ago that I'm gay, and we haven't really dealt with it. But we need to now. Charlie is the person I want to date."

"Charlie's not a boy?"

"No."

"Charlie's a girl?"

"No."

"I don't understand."

"Charlie's genderqueer, Nana, and we call Charlie 'they.'"

"What does that mean?"

"I'm not entirely sure, but I know I want to find out more, and I know we need to respect it. Once you meet Charlie, you'll love them."

"And this Charlie makes you happy?"

I grinned. "I think they will."

Nana made a fussy old lady gesture that was a cross between a shrug and a "fuck you." It was her way of saying she didn't really understand, but if I was happy, whatever. She'd figure it out. We all would. She picked up her fork and took another teeny bite of sesame chicken. I picked up my eggroll, glad for the chance to finish it and pretend it wasn't my fourth.

"Did you say you quit your job?" Nana asked suddenly.

"Uh...maybe?"

"Do you have another lined up?"

"Uh...'Lined up' as in I have an interview and an offer, or 'lined up' as in there's a plan in my brain?"

Her wrinkled maroon lips pursed. She was disappointed in me. And that was why I'd held off on the biggest news. It was my way of spinning a potentially negative and probably foolhardy decision into a positive choice that reflected my deep, abiding commitment to my elderly grandmother. Once she heard the rest, she wouldn't be able to stay angry at me.

"I want to move back here."

As I predicted, dinner was fairly smooth after that. The prodigal grandchild was returning home, and nothing else I did or said mattered. Coming home broke without a car? No big deal. Dating a nonbinary pig farmer? Totally fine. All Nana really wanted was to have me around.

She perked up and praised me, and I basked in it. As we continued to eat, she talked about where I should move and what my apartment budget should be, conveniently neglecting that I'd told her I had no money and no job. She'd probably pay the deposit and first month's rent if it meant having a vote in where I lived. Knowing my relationship with family money, which was that I was more dependent on it than I wanted to be and minded way less about that dependence than I ought to have, I probably wouldn't refuse Nana's help.

When we finished eating, the check arrived on a plastic tray with miniature fruit candies. I took the lemon one and gave Nana the raspberry. As we slid out of the booth, I told her, "I have a date with Charlie tonight. Do you want to meet them?"

It wasn't cool of me to put that off until the last second. It was already 8:30, so if Nana had said that no, she didn't want to meet Charlie, I wasn't sure what I would have done. Charlie was planning to be at our house in thirty minutes. Nana usually went to bed between nine and ten, but I hadn't asked her what her plans for the night were or if she minded Charlie coming over. I was being selfish. I wanted them to meet, and I put them both in a position where they had no choice.

When we got back to the house, Nana decided to make a pot of tea. I left her clattering around the kitchen while I awaited Charlie anxiously. At two minutes past nine, I saw headlights turn into the short driveway. Charlie had driven the reindeer antler SUV again, and I wondered how long after Christmas the Barlows would keep those dumb things suction-cupped to the car. I came outside to greet them, and we immediately kissed.

"Your car looks so stupid," I couldn't help saying.

"Says the one with no car." Charlie's hand was still resting on the back of my neck, and they leaned in for another quick kiss. "What's the plan?"

"Um." I felt like a teenager asking a date to come inside to deal with my dad and his hard-nosed attitude of "What is your intention with my daughter?" when all Ben Fischer had wanted to do was honk and have me come out because who wanted to deal with a threatening dad if you didn't even like the girl that much? "Do you want to meet my Nana?"

"Hell yes. Lead the way."

Beaming, I brought Charlie into the house. Nana was in her nightgown and robe. She was a fairly stylish old lady. No shapeless flannel housedresses for her. It was a long coral silk gown with a matching silk robe and slippers. She still had her lipstick on, which I guessed was her way of making herself "presentable for company." She was waiting for us in the living room, where she'd put out a tray of cookies and the pot of tea.

"I love her," Charlie murmured to me as we took in the scene.

I wasn't sure if Nana would love Charlie, and I prayed she wouldn't do or say something offensive. Nana was the kind of Democrat who would live and die for the party's platform, and she liked to think her beliefs were progressive. The reality was that because of generational differences, she sometimes said things ignorantly, not knowing that certain words or phrases were no longer considered acceptable. And the twenty-first century had brought out into the open a lot of ideas, like being queer instead of regular gay, that were foreign to her.

"You're Charlie," Nana announced.

Charlie immediately stuck their hand out for a shake. "I am, ma'am, and I'm really happy to meet you, though I have to say that Dana's never told me your name. I only know you as Nana."

Nana shook Charlie's hand as if it were a job interview before seating herself imperiously in one of the chairs opposite the couch. Charlie and I sat side by side on the couch, and I immediately reached for a cookie covered in red sprinkles. Nothing like avoiding awkward moments by cramming food into one's mouth.

"You can call me Nana," I heard my grandmother say. My best friend Rachel Bromberg in high school had called her "Nana," but Rachel had spent most of her free time with my family while her own parents jetted off around the world or stayed late at the office for special board meetings that Rachel and I always suspected were covers for torrid affairs with colleagues. We had been inseparable, so it made sense that Rachel would consider my grandmother her own. She'd called my parents by their first names, Aaron and Abby, but in our junior year she had given my mother a bouquet of tulips for Mother's Day. I doubted she'd given her own mother anything.

Rachel and I had drifted apart when we went to separate colleges. She'd come to my parents' funeral, and we'd had a chance to catch up. She was married and pregnant before the ink on our college diplomas was dry, and I was a lesbian with an attitude, and it had been clear there wasn't a lot left to keep our friendship going. Now I wondered how she was doing. Maybe she was still in the area, and I could reconnect with her again.

In the present, Charlie was telling Nana about the pigs, only when Charlie talked about it, it sounded a lot less like that scary scene in *The Wizard of Oz* when Dorothy fell into the pig pen and more like a futuristic science lab. I wondered if Nana understood much of what Charlie was talking about. I certainly didn't. The most I could understand was that Charlie tried to feed the pigs very, very healthy food to keep them alive as long as possible.

If health was what they valued, they were going to be horrified to find out that I'd crammed four fried eggrolls down my throat at dinner.

I tuned back in to hear them both laughing about me.

"What'd I miss?"

"Dane, I'm trying to picture you in that tree costume," Charlie said with mirth.

Oh no. Nana had told Charlie about my preschool class play. Why on earth would she do that? I had been assigned to be a tree in the enchanted forest. My job had been to swing branches for the explorers, the kids who were the stars of our little show, to play on. I'd ended up smacking one of them in the face, and he'd started crying, and then I'd looked to the wings for guidance from our preschool teacher. She'd kept making the swaying motion, so I smacked the little girl, that time on purpose. Some of the parents in the audience had laughed, and some had yelled. At four, I hadn't understood what I'd done wrong, since we'd been coached for weeks to look at the teacher if we forgot what to do, and I'd done exactly what she had shown me.

Looking at the photos from that illustrious foray into acting, I had later learned that the back of my brown tree trunk tights had been tucked into my white underwear. When I'd finally turned around to flee the stage, the whole audience had seen my panties.

Come to think of it, I had a knack for accidentally showing my bum.

"I could tell embarrassing stories about you, too, Nana," I said grumpily. "And, Charlie, don't think I haven't forgotten about your theatrical visits to Denny's." A thought occurred to me. "Wait a second, was *Clint* the one with the crutches?"

Charlie nodded. "He's a different person now. Much more settled."

But still loud and flamboyant, from what I'd seen. I explained to Nana, "Clint was Charlie's best friend in college. I met him last night when we were trying to get home, and I met him again this afternoon. He's nice."

"Maybe now you'll have some friends," Nana said candidly. She rose from the chair. "I'm off to bed. You two don't stay up too late."

I kissed her good night even though she didn't deserve it for that remark. "I have friends," I told Charlie.

"Sure, you've got me and your grandmother and good old Mitchell Wormerstein."

As Nana began the slow trudge up the stairs, she turned over her shoulder. "Be good!"

"We definitely won't be!" Charlie called back.

I gasped, but to my surprise, I could hear Nana laughing.

Once she was gone, I became aware of how bright the room was, how small the couch was, and how full of expectation this moment was.

Charlie crossed their legs, the right ankle resting atop the bony knee of their left leg. They gave their pants a little tug and gazed toward the kitchen. They were nervous, too. "So what's going on?"

"What do you mean?"

"You're nervous or something."

"I'm not nervous. I just didn't appreciate being the brunt of all the jokes."

Charlie called me out. "You loved it. You're mildly embarrassed, but you like hearing stories about yourself, and you like that your Nana and I got along."

"I do not like hearing stories about myself, and it hardly matters if you and Nana got along, if you and I don't." I was smarting from being teased by the two of them and didn't mean it, but in the stark light and quiet of the living room, Charlie heard my tone differently.

"Dana, if you're having second thoughts about this, you should say so."

"No! God, no! Not at all!"

"Okay, then...What's really going on?"

"I told you."

"No, I mean, something serious is bothering you. You can tell me. I want to hear what's on your mind."

I sighed. We'd had our nice romantic moment at the coffee shop, and now we'd done the meeting the grandparent bit. It was time to come clean about all the serious things.

"You got your trust fund back," I began slowly, each word rolling around my mouth.

"I did."

"I...think that...you...think that I feel like...you—"

"Dane, you've already lost me with all the thinking and feeling."

I cleared my throat again. Breathed in, out, opened my mouth to speak, and began, "I'm not a spoiled rich kid!"

Charlie leaned forward to grab a cookie and ate it, cocking an eyebrow at me as they did.

"Okay, fine, I will always be a spoiled rich kid," I conceded. "But I'm not rich on my own. My job didn't actually pay that much, and...see, the thing that I haven't told you and feel like shit that I haven't told you is…I quit it. And I can't afford to replace my car. I'm totally broke."

I waited for Charlie to interject, but they didn't.

"You hate me, don't you? You lost all your attraction to me. Why aren't you saying anything? Can you please say something? I'm dying here."

"Money or not, I'm still the same person. You're still the same person. Aren't you?" Charlie finished the cookie. "What else?"

"There's nothing else," I lied.

"Dane, you know what would be great to me? If we made an oath for total honesty. I think one of the huge problems I've had with exes in the past—"

"With Caroline," I corrected them.

"Is that we withheld too many things from each other. When you feel comfortable, I would really like it if you told me what else you were thinking and feeling."

It was hard to resist that invitation. *When you feel comfortable.* Not, *Dana, I demand you to speak*, but, *Dana, it would mean a lot to me if you would share with me.*

How did you tell someone you had no idea how to touch their body? It was like being a virgin all over again. At age thirty-two. In typical Dana fashion, I was overthinking the whole thing, and that was probably making it worse. Also in typical Dana fashion, I didn't know how to express it, except to just blurt it out.

"I don't know if I'm allowed to touch your boobs!" I buried my face in my hands, mortified.

Charlie didn't comfort me, and that made it all worse. I didn't want to blow this. I wanted to get it right, for both our sakes, but I didn't know how to do that without talking about some really uncomfortable things.

I split the fingers of one hand into a V and peeked out. "Charlie, please say something. You're always the one who knows what to say and do in situations like this."

"Yeah, I know, but you have to understand that I'm just as sensitive about body stuff as you, and it puts a lot of pressure on me to have to express it."

"I know." I didn't.

"People ask me about my body all the time, Dane. Whether I've had surgery, whether I want to get surgery, which parts I have under my clothes. People have tried to have sex with me just to see what's down there."

That sounded horrifying. I couldn't imagine how awful that made Charlie feel. I wouldn't have guessed things like that happened, and I didn't want Charlie to think that's what I was doing.

"That's not what this is for me."

"I know," Charlie said quietly. "I know that's why you're nervous. I know—I think, anyway, that this is about more than the thrill of seeing my body and getting to tell stories about it."

Who would I even tell?

"It's not even close to that."

"You remember how you felt when we saw that accident?"

The comparison registered to me. Car accidents triggered panic in me, but car accidents, I knew logically, were going to happen. Not every accident meant death. Sometimes people just tapped each other when they didn't stop fast enough at a red light. It didn't have to mean losing my shit. I guessed what Charlie was trying to explain was that talking about their body induced the same kind of terror in them. Maybe Charlie knew that I had questions because I wanted to do justice to this new thing between us, and maybe Charlie understood intellectually that I was trustworthy. But none of that meant Charlie had control over their panic at being used.

How tiring to always have to explain one's identity, one's body, one's sexuality. I could barely handle having to tell Nana every Christmas that I didn't want to find a nice man and settle down. Nana had never asked me about my private parts.

"What would make the body stuff easier?" I asked.

"Could we not talk about it? Just…feel it out in the moment? What do you want to do?"

"I want to make love to you," I said, not caring if it sounded cheesy. "I want it to be hot and sexy, but I also think I could trust you. And I think that being together with you will feel nice."

"It's always better when you have an emotional connection," Charlie agreed.

"What do you want to do?"

I could hear the silk covering of the couch rustle. Charlie pulled my hands away from my face. I saw nothing but desire and trust in their eyes. The swagger was back.

"I want to rock your world," they said, leaning close. "And I want to find out what makes you tick."

My breath was coming fast. I was leaning back against the arm of the couch now, and Charlie was hovering above me. I needed to feel the weight of their body on mine, the contact of our skin. "And I can find out what makes you tick back?"

"You got it," Charlie breathed, punctuating the line with a heavy kiss.

Chapter Fifteen

We did not have sex on Nana's couch. That would have been weird for a lot of reasons. We found our way to my bedroom, which was removed from Nana's by another bedroom and a bathroom. I still felt we were in the weird zone. I'd never had sex in that house or anywhere in the vicinity of parental figures. When I was in college, all the action happened in the dorms, and I'd refrained on winter and summer breaks. Call me prudish.

Which is exactly what Charlie did, only they breathed the word over my nude torso teasingly. If that was the kind of punishment prudes got, I hardly minded.

I learned a lot about Charlie that night. It was the most fun, least nerve-wracking sex I had ever had. We guided each other's hands to places that wanted to be touched, we kissed and held each other at times, and at other times we threw our bodies against each other in frenetic rhythm. All my questions about what Charlie liked and how Charlie's body worked were answered naturally. And the same back for me. Charlie took their time lovingly exploring my body and finding all the points at which I squirmed and panted and begged for them to stop, not meaning a word of it and actually pleading for more.

It was the best sex of my life.

When it was over, we were breathless and sweaty and sated. As I held Charlie in a tight spoon, I kissed the back of their neck in reassurance that it had been about more than our bodies and that much more was to come.

But, if I was moving back here and Charlie was still in Indiana, when?

Charlie sensed there was something bothering me. They turned on their side, propped their head on an elbow, and gave me an anticipatory look.

This must have been what they meant by "pillow talk."

I lay back and stared at the still ceiling fan. "How do you always know? Why is it so hard to hide things from you?"

"You're easy to read."

"Yeah, well," I groused, "I recall saying the same thing about you yesterday when we were engaged."

I definitely did not mention our fake engagement because I wanted to think about the possibility of now being for-real engaged. Nope. No connection there at all, not even a subconscious one. We were way too new for that.

But how sweet it would be to have that kind of commitment from Charlie, to know that they'd love and support me through thick and thin. To have a ring on my finger, and every time I looked at it, I would think of them. Everyone who saw it would know it signified our relationship. I was old-fashioned. For some of my friends, marriage was out of the picture, a non-starter that represented the heteronormative chains being queer supposedly liberated us from. Not me. I didn't want to wear a lacy white dress and walk down the aisle to "Here Comes the Bride" or Pachelbel's *Canon in D*. I just wanted someone to hold my hand while we were out shopping and remember my birthday and keep me warm at night. And I wanted to do all those things back for someone. I wanted someone to call me their wife.

"Any day now, Dane," Charlie prodded gently. "I hate to kill the post-sex buzz, but I do have to get home at some point. My dad's going to need the car to get to work."

Rushing home from sex so Dad could take the car to work was the worst walk of shame imaginable. Did their dad know they had the car? Did he know the car was taken in pursuit of sex? Would he think we'd had sex inside the car? I'd never be able to face him again.

Also, I didn't want Charlie to rush home. I wanted Charlie to languish in bed with me until we ventured downstairs for coffee and pancakes. Or maybe out to brunch. Once Charlie left, the little honeymoon would be over, and the realities of a long-distance relationship would kick in.

"Don't go," I pouted.

"I don't want to, but I'm going to have to eventually. We can spend the time we have left staring at the ceiling, or you can tell me what's up."

"We can't have sex again?" My petulance wasn't real. As much as I wanted to be with Charlie, I doubted I had the energy for another round. Maybe it was time to make a New Year's resolution to up my cardio workouts.

Charlie tweaked my nipple. "I'd love to. Tell me what's going on first."

"You know," I pointed out, "before we had sex, you were really nice about me not wanting to talk. You were all, 'When you're ready, Dana. It would mean so much to me if you confided in me, Dana.' Now that you've had your way with me, it's all demands."

"Hardly."

"Remember how you said you wanted total honesty?"

"Mm-hm."

"I feel like I lied to you all day yesterday and today about something."

"Oh, no, what? Your car didn't actually break down, but you just wanted a ride because you thought I was hot?"

"No! I mean, you're hot, but, be serious."

"You're married?"

"No!"

"You hate pigs?" They clapped their hands lightly. "That's what's been bothering you this whole time. You hate pigs."

"I have yet to see evidence of your pigs," I reminded them. "We went to your house, and there wasn't even a…what do you call it? Pig pen?"

"Sty?" Charlie made a face. "You know I'm not a farmer, right?"

"Yeah, of course, you do research. With pigs. Pig research. Agricultural pig research." It was pretty evident I had no idea what that meant.

Charlie leaned over the edge of the bed, giving me a nice view of their ivory back and perfectly round bum. They returned with their cell phone. "You wanna see photos?"

There was so much pride in their voice that I couldn't say no. They showed me an album of photos, some of big fat porkers flopping around straw in the sun, some of Charlie nose to snout with one of them. Charlie was smiling, the telltale selfie arm reflected in their mirrored sunglasses, and there was no concern at all on their face that touching pigs might be kind of gross. In others, someone else had photographed Charlie in the lab with a pig. The pig's dusty pink skin contrasted the gleaming stainless steel underneath their hooves and the bright, crisp white of Charlie's lab coat.

"They're…cute? Where's all the mud?"

"Aren't they? They get to wallow sometimes when they're hot outside, but they're usually very cool indoors, and they like being clean."

"You have a lab coat?"

"Of course, it's standard daily wear. I'm not a farmer, Dane. I'm a scientist."

Charlie had said as much the day before, but it hadn't really registered until I saw the lab coat and sterile environment in which they worked. If Charlie was a scientist, that explained the lack of stables and crops around their cabin, and my image of a scientist meshed better with the velvet blazer and the trust fund. But science lab Charlie was a far cry from the rusty pickup truck and the Carhartt jacket and the rugged attitude. I wondered if I'd ever finish peeling back the layers that made Charlie who they were.

They swiped across the phone a few more times, admiring their own photos. "This is Delphina. She's such a brat. Reminds me of you."

"Cute." Neither the pig nor the comparison was cute, but it would have been bad form to pretend otherwise.

"And this is Jorge. He fell off a pig truck and was rescued by someone driving down the highway behind the truck. They brought him to us because the local shelter doesn't take non-domesticated animals. We got him when he was still a piglet, and now he's two, which is kind of amazing for an American Yorkshire. He'd have been slaughtered at six months if he hadn't gotten rescued."

"Wait, they kill pigs when they're six months old? That's so young!"

"Yep."

I was never eating bacon again.

"What do you do with him?" I wondered. "If he's so old?"

"He's not in research. We just keep him for unsponsored, unofficial training research and our own entertainment."

"Like what?"

"I've taught him to sit, shake, spin, and oink on command."

"Pigs can do that? Like dogs?"

"Oh yeah," Charlie explained. "They're very intelligent, and they love working for treats. The idea that pigs want to lie around being fat and lazy comes entirely from industrial farming. They're happy to have things to do." Charlie showed me another photo. The pink piggy was pushing a soccer ball with his nose. "I'm teaching him how to score a goal."

"You really love them, don't you?" Charlie didn't need to answer. It was obvious in the way they took a million photos and wanted to show them to me. Charlie had their place, and that was in Indiana with their research and their pigs.

I didn't have a place, and that's why I was moving. "So here's what's been bothering me," I said. "I think yesterday helped me to realize I'm not happy at all in Cleveland. I don't have any meaningful friendships. I don't have a dog or a pig. I didn't even like my job. I think I liked pretending, you know? Getting dressed every morning and getting my coffee on the way to work. I thought it would be glamorous working at the art museum, but my job was just begging rich people for money and feeling demeaned when they made demands before they'd give it. I think I've been trying really hard to convince myself that I had everything I wanted, but what I had was a bunch of stuff that doesn't even matter."

Charlie was quiet for a moment, processing what I'd said. Then they nodded sagely. "How did you figure that out?"

Were they seriously asking? Did they not understand how significant my day with them had been?

"Charlie, you made me see what it was like to feel loved and appreciated. No one's ever made me feel that way before." Charlie gave me a happy smile at that. "Plus, we just…it was such a stupid day, and it was awful, but it was also kind of fun. I felt like we were on this adventure together."

I don't want the adventure to stop. I couldn't say the words out loud. I was too nervous and too aware that in a few days, we'd part ways. Our lives were already in different states, and with my move, they'd be hundreds of miles apart.

"If you're not happy in Cleveland," Charlie asked, "where would you be happy?" Their voice was tinged with hope. Maybe they wanted me to say I'd move in with them, but what would I do in the middle of Indiana? I wouldn't know anyone, and I had no idea what kind of job I could find. Besides, as much as I didn't want to let Charlie go, I didn't want to blow this by rushing to move in together out of convenience. I'd rushed relationships before, and they'd crashed and burned that much faster. I wanted this to start on a sturdy foundation, and I wanted to enjoy those heady early days when everything is new and sizzling.

"I don't want to live so far away from Nana." I watched their face carefully to see if they looked disappointed. They didn't. Good. It wasn't as if I announced I was moving to California or Maine. Now that Charlie had reconciled with their parents, surely they planned to visit more often, and we could see each other. I continued my rationale. "I don't want to look back in five years, ten years, however long Nana has left, and think that I spent it working some dumb job I didn't care about four hundred miles and three states away."

"You want to live here?"

I shrugged. "Probably not on the North Shore. I was thinking downtown. But maybe I should live in Nana's house and take better care of her. Do you know she calls a transportation service to go to the salon?"

"She has great hair," Charlie observed.

"Yeah, but why should she go to that trouble and expense? Couldn't I do that for her?" I sighed and flopped onto my stomach, propping myself up, too. Charlie tucked a loose strand of my hair behind my ear. "I'm starting to realize that all the things I've missed with my own parents, well, I'm missing them with Nana, and I don't have to. She's still here and needs me, and I'm not saying I shouldn't have a life of my own. I guess I just mean that I don't want to look back on this time and regret my choices."

"I think I know what you mean," Charlie answered slowly. "Since my parents told me they want to make up, I can't stop thinking about what it will be like to leave in a few days. I want to keep working on stuff with them. I owe you for making me give them a chance. I wouldn't have done it without you."

"How did it go tonight?"

"Dad's still super weird. I think he believes he's getting a son or something."

"But you have two brothers." I tried to remember their names from our quick introductions. "Joe and...?"

"Joe's okay. Dad's very pleased that he and Carly got married, though I know Mom thinks they were too young. It was right out of college. They don't want to have any kids, and I know my parents are sad about that."

"Who's the other one?" I asked. "I'm sorry I can't remember. I just remember Horty because, you know, *Horty*."

"Her name is Hortense, but that's not much better," Charlie said. "My younger brother is Pete."

"Yeah, Pete, okay. Why doesn't your dad consider him a son?"

"Petey's totally gay. I know it, Dad knows it, nobody talks about it. I just don't know if *Pete* knows it yet."

"Oh no," I laughed. "Maybe you being so open will help him."

"I hope so," Charlie said seriously. "I suspect that's part of the reason why my parents were so hard on me. I think they thought my queerness had a ripple effect."

"That's not how it works."

"I know that, and you know that, but who knows if Lydia and Preston know that? I think part of the reason Petey hasn't accepted who he is yet is because he saw how my parents reacted to me. When he was in high school and I was in college, he used to try to tag along with me and Clint all the time. So did Caroline. I thought it was annoying, but Clint always said we should be nice to our baby queer siblings."

"And look how that turned out!" I hadn't meant to sound venomous, but damn. Was there a time when Charlie and Clint could have avoided helping Caroline discover her identity and therefore prevent Caroline and Charlie from ever being an item? How could we transport to that universe?

"How about you? Did your parents freak out when you came out? Were they around for that?" Charlie put a hand on my arm to forestall a response. "Hang on, let me ask you something first. Is it okay to ask you questions about them?"

I smiled. "Yes. Thank you for asking me. I know some people think that if they talk about my parents, it'll make me sad. The truth is, I'm always sad, they're always dead, and I'm never not thinking about them. I welcome the chance to talk about them, to keep their memories alive."

Charlie smiled back. "I wish I could meet them."

"I'd like to think they'd like you. To answer your question, they were around when I came out. They did freak out a little," I admitted, "but they had become super supportive by the time they died. Thankfully. I don't know how I would feel to have lost them when we didn't get along. Nana, though, she tries to fix me up every year. You walked in on this year's efforts."

"Good old Mitch who you were flirting with?" Charlie asked pointedly.

"I was not flirting with good old Mitch."

"Did you ever think that maybe you're not a lesbian?" Before I could protest, Charlie held up their hands placatingly. "Okay, okay, you should be able to call yourself whatever you want. I just meant that maybe you're not only entirely attracted to cis lesbian women."

Charlie had a point there. I had most certainly not flirted with Mitchell Wormerstein, but I had appreciated, from a reserved aesthetic position, how attractive he was. And I was attracted to Charlie, who was not a woman. However Charlie had been raised and however their body looked in private, it didn't move like or desire the same kind of touch as a cis lesbian.

"I guess I'll just say I'm queer from now on," I said tentatively. The word still conjured images of protesting the system in ways that didn't seem fitting to boring old me. I didn't have any piercings, but I did have money in the stock market. Sexuality was a journey, though. I had learned that from my college alliance group. It was okay not to know one's identity, and it was okay for that identity to change. That was part of growing as a person.

"How come you called Pete gay, but you just said people get to decide their own labels?" I asked. "And what do you think will happen if he does come out? Do you think your parents will disown him too?"

"I don't think so. I think my parents are working hard to be more accepting. And who knows? Maybe Pete will end up with Clint. That's kind of been a fantasy of mine."

"If that doesn't work out," I suggested, "there's always Mitchell Wormerstein."

Charlie grinned and put a hand reverently on my back. "You're mine, not good old Mitch's." The feminist in me was supposed to chafe at the idea of belonging to someone, but the primal growl in Charlie's voice only awakened my most fervent desires.

"I want to keep being yours." My throat caught as I fumbled to explain the problem I foresaw. "Is this totally stupid to think—but Cleveland is closer to you and the pigs, and I know I just met you, but I've never felt so comfortable and safe. I don't want to give that up, you know? I want to see where this is going."

"I want to see where this is going, too. I actually have something to tell you, too."

"You do?"

"Uh…" Charlie wouldn't make eye contact, which I knew meant something big was coming. I couldn't think what. "This morning, I actually did some research online."

"What kind of research?"

"There's an animal research center connected to the Ohio State University that's only about an hour away from Cleveland."

"You looked up places where you could work near me?" They nodded. "Charlie, that's...wow."

"But if you're going to be here..."

"Yeah?"

"I actually looked around to see what kind of jobs there are in the area, and it's possible here. So if you're going to be here, and my family is here, and I want to be close to you and to them..."

In classic Dana fashion, I didn't really hear them. I kept rambling on. "I don't have a car, so I'm not even sure how I'm going to get home. Maybe Nana and I have to buy one tomorrow? But I don't even have enough money in savings for a down payment. I mean, I can find the money—I don't want you to think I'm poor or anything, I know I was borrowing money from you yesterday, but that was different—"

"Dana?"

"Yeah?"

"Do you want to move home with me?"

"Really?"

"Really. What do you think?"

"You can do that? What about Jorge and Delphina?"

Charlie shrugged. "There's a lot of details to work out, and it's not as if I can just walk into a lab and get a job, but I would like to try to sort through those details. Would you?"

I grinned. "Yeah."

Charlie slid one hand around the nape of my neck, and as we leaned into the kiss, I felt all my worries wash away. The kiss was a pledge that they liked me and that maybe they were starting to fall in love with me. The kiss told me not to worry, and I knew that however the rest of this Christmas adventure went, we would figure it out together.

CHAPTER SIXTEEN

"Are you sure you have everything?" Nana asked for the tenth time.

I tried not to roll my eyes and reminded myself she was only asking because she cared. "Yes, Nana."

I looked at the heap of bags by her front door. My new purse, which we'd bought the day after Christmas at a mega sale; my old purse, which had been rescued from Charlie's truck two days after Christmas when the tow lot reopened, and which miraculously still had my wallet inside it; my suitcase, thankfully protected from the snow and sleet by the tarp Charlie had stretched across the truck's flatbed; and, of course, Charlie's things.

Charlie came back inside to fetch another load. "Did you remember to get those audiobooks?"

I had wanted to download them to my phone, but the truck wasn't technologically advanced enough to route my phone through its speakers. In a rumbly old truck, there was no way we'd hear off the phone itself. I'd opted instead for Charlie's preferred bargain basement audiobook CDs. The drive to Cleveland was supposed to take six hours, not counting bathroom and gas stops, but I'd bought three books, a total of twelve hours of materials. No way was I going to get stuck listening to Christmas music that would probably still be on the air even though Christmas had already come and gone.

"I got 'em."

"Are we taking any food?"

I tried to shush her, but I wasn't fast enough.

"Food!" Nana exclaimed. "Good idea. Let me pack you a lunch." She shuffled to the kitchen, Charlie mouthed that they were sorry, and I wondered if we were ever going to hit the road.

By the time Nana returned a few minutes later with three plastic storage containers of sandwiches and Christmas cookies, Charlie had everything loaded into the back of the truck and secured with the tarp. They smiled widely at Nana's offerings, which they probably couldn't even eat because they weren't vegan, thanked her, and kissed her on the cheek.

They had known each other four days, and they were already acting like grandmother and grandchild.

"All right, can we finally go?" I asked. "We have a long drive ahead, and if we don't leave right now, we might not get to Cleveland before the movers arrive."

We had stayed longer with our families than we had planned. It had given us time to get to know each other and given Charlie time to reconnect with their parents. Now, though, we had to race to Cleveland in time to pack my apartment. Then we'd turn around and do the same thing at Charlie's. The lab and the pigs would have to wait a few weeks to be wrapped up. Charlie thought it would be detrimental to leave Jorge and some of the others in Indiana, since they had bonded. I had learned that pigs can form deep emotional attachments to humans. They couldn't quit their job without sufficient time to wrap up projects, so they'd have to commute for a while. But that would be sorted out after we rushed back to Chicago in time for Clint's New Year's Eve party. I couldn't wait to kiss Charlie at midnight.

"Yes, yes," Charlie said. "Let me go to the bathroom quick."

I put my hands on my hips impatiently.

"And you'll be back on your birthday?" Nana asked again.

We had already gone over the logistics myriad times, but she was either too forgetful or too nervous.

"Yes," I promised. "I will be back for the new year." My birthday was a few days after that, and I was really excited to spend it with Nana for once. And having a new "goyfriend" was going to make this birthday even better. We'd settled on the term "goyfriend" because it was a mashup of "girlfriend" and "boyfriend" but also because Charlie was a goy, as in not Jewish. We thought it was funny.

"I can't believe you're moving back home." Nana squeezed my cheeks. "My sweet girl."

I smiled fondly at her. "I can't believe it either." After college, all I had wanted was to get away, to show my independence and go find a life for myself somewhere else. Now all I wanted was to hurry back to Cleveland because the faster I got there, the faster I could get back to this new life I was going to make in Chicago with Charlie. Neither of us knew yet where we were going to live, and neither of us had a job yet. But for the moment, we were financially solvent, and, more importantly, we had the love and support of both families.

Charlie came out of the bathroom, and I resisted the urge to yell, "Finally!" They put their arm around my waist, a natural gesture that showed how much they thought of us as a team. "You ready?"

On the way to Christmas in Highland Park, I'd driven alone, the cold air of the empty passenger seat swallowing up the energy in the car. Now I would drive back with a partner, someone who, after only a few days, was going to uproot their life for me, and I was going to do the same. It was crazy. It was romantic. It felt right.

"I'm ready."

The End

About the Author

Jane Kolven is an author of contemporary, fun LGBTQ romances. She is proud to create stories that show a variety of LGBTQ people finding happiness—because everyone deserves love. Jane currently lives in Michigan with her wife and their pets.

Books Available from Bold Strokes Books

Bet Against Me by Fiona Riley. In the high stakes luxury real estate market, everything has a price, and as rival Realtors Trina Lee and Kendall Yates find out, that means their hearts and souls, too. (978-1-63555-729-9)

Broken Reign by Sam Ledel. Together on an epic journey in search of a mysterious cure, a princess and a village outcast must overcome life-threatening challenges and their own prejudice if they want to survive. (978-1-63555-739-8)

Just One Taste by CJ Birch. For Lauren, it only took one taste to start trusting in love again. (978-1-63555-772-5)

Lady of Stone by Barbara Ann Wright. Sparks fly as a magical emergency forces a noble embarrassed by her ability to submit to a low-born teacher who resents everything about her. (978-1-63555-607-0)

Last Resort by Angie Williams. Katie and Rhys are about to find out what happens when you meet the girl of your dreams but you aren't looking for a happily ever after. (978-1-63555-774-9)

Longing for You by Jenny Frame. When Debrek housekeeper Katie Brekman is attacked amid a burgeoning vampire-witch war, Alexis Villiers must go against everything her clan believes in to save her. (978-1-63555-658-2)

Money Creek by Anne Laughlin. Clare Lehane is a troubled lawyer from Chicago who tries to make her way in a rural town full of secrets and deceptions. (978-1-63555-795-4)

Passion's Sweet Surrender by Ronica Black. Cam and Blake are unable to deny their passion for each other, but surrendering to love is a whole different matter. (978-1-63555-703-9)

The Holiday Detour by Jane Kolven. It will take everything going wrong to make Dana and Charlie see how right they are for each other. (978-1-63555-720-6)

Too Hot to Ride by Andrews & Austin. World famous cutting horse champion and industry legend Jane Barrow is knockdown sexy in the way she moves, talks, and rides, and Rae Starr is determined not to get involved with this womanizing gambler. (978-1-63555-776-3)

A Love that Leads to Home by Ronica Black. For Carla Sims and Janice Carpenter, home isn't about location, it's where your heart is. (978-1-63555-675-9)

Blades of Bluegrass by D. Jackson Leigh. A US Army occupational therapist must rehab a bitter veteran who is a ticking political time bomb the military is desperate to disarm. (978-1-63555-637-7)

Guarding Hearts by Jaycie Morrison. As treachery and temptation threaten the women of the Women's Army Corps, who will risk it all for love? (978-1-63555-806-7)

Hopeless Romantic by Georgia Beers. Can a jaded wedding planner and an optimistic divorce attorney possibly find a future together? (978-1-63555-650-6)

Hopes and Dreams by PJ Trebelhorn. Movie theater manager Riley Warren is forced to face her high school crush and tormentor, wealthy socialite Victoria Thayer, at their twentieth reunion. (978-1-63555-670-4)

In the Cards by Kimberly Cooper Griffin. Daria and Phaedra are about to discover that love finds a way, especially when powers outside their control are at play. (978-1-63555-717-6)

Moon Fever by Ileandra Young. SPEAR agent Danika Karson must clear her werewolf friend of multiple false charges while teaching her vampire girlfriend to resist the blood mania brought on by a full moon. (978-1-63555-603-2)

Quake City by St John Karp. Can Andre find his best friend Amy before the night devolves into a nightmare of broken hearts, malevolent drag queens, and spontaneous human combustion? Or has it always happened this way, every night, at Aunty Bob's Quake City Club? (978-1-63555-723-7)

Serenity by Jesse J. Thoma. For Kit Marsden, there are many things in life she cannot change. Serenity is in the acceptance. (978-1-63555-713-8)

Sylver and Gold by Michelle Larkin. Working feverishly to find a killer before he strikes again, Boston Homicide Detective Reid Sylver and rookie cop London Gold are blindsided by their chemistry and developing attraction. (978-1-63555-611-7)

Trade Secrets by Kathleen Knowles. In Silicon Valley, love and business are a volatile mix for clinical lab scientist Tony Leung and venture capitalist Sheila Graham. (978-1-63555-642-1)

Death Overdue by David S. Pederson. Did Heath turn to murder in an alcohol induced haze to solve the problem of his blackmailer, or was it someone else who brought about a death overdue? (978-1-63555-711-4)

Entangled by Melissa Brayden. Becca Crawford is the perfect person to head up the Jade Hotel, if only the captivating owner of the local vineyard would get on board with her plan and stop badmouthing the hotel to everyone in town. (978-1-63555-709-1)

First Do No Harm by Emily Smith. Pierce and Cassidy are about to discover that when it comes to love, sometimes you have to risk it all to have it all. (978-1-63555-699-5)

Kiss Me Every Day by Dena Blake. For Wynn Evans, wishing for a do-over with Carly Jamison was a long shot, actually getting one was a game changer. (978-1-63555-551-6)

Olivia by Genevieve McCluer. In this lesbian Shakespeare adaptation with vampires, Olivia is a centuries old vampire who must fight a strange figure from her past if she wants a chance at happiness. (978-1-63555-701-5)

One Woman's Treasure by Jean Copeland. Daphne's search for discarded antiques and treasures leads to an embarrassing misunderstanding, and ultimately, the opportunity for the romance of a lifetime with Nina. (978-1-63555-652-0)

Silver Ravens by Jane Fletcher. Lori has lost her girlfriend, her home, and her job. Things don't improve when she's kidnapped and taken to fairyland. (978-1-63555-631-5)

Still Not Over You by Jenny Frame, Carsen Taite, Ali Vali. Old flames die hard in these tales of a second chance at love with the ex you're still not over. Stories by award winning authors Jenny Frame, Carsen Taite, and Ali Vali. (978-1-63555-516-5)

Storm Lines by Jessica L. Webb. Devon is a psychologist who likes rules. Marley is a cop who doesn't. They don't always agree, but both fight to protect a girl immersed in a street drug ring. (978-1-63555-626-1)

The Politics of Love by Jen Jensen. Is it possible to love across the political divide in a hostile world? Conservative Shelley Whitmore and liberal Rand Thomas are about to find out. (978-1-63555-693-3)

All the Paths to You by Morgan Lee Miller. High school sweethearts Quinn Hughes and Kennedy Reed reconnect five years after they break up and realize that their chemistry is all but over. (978-1-63555-662-9)

Arrested Pleasures by Nanisi Barrett D'Arnuck. When charged with a crime she didn't commit, Katherine Lowe faces the question: Which is harder, going to prison or falling in love? (978-1-63555-684-1)

Bonded Love by Renee Roman. Carpenter Blaze Carter suffers an injury that shatters her dreams, and ER nurse Trinity Greene hopes to show her that sometimes love is worth fighting for. (978-1-63555-530-1)

Convergence by Jane C. Esther. With life as they know it on the line, can Aerin McLeary and Olivia Ando's love survive an otherworldly threat to humankind? (978-1-63555-488-5)

Coyote Blues by Karen F. Williams. Riley Dawson, psychotherapist and shape-shifter, has her world turned upside down when Fiona Bell, her one true love, returns. (978-1-63555-558-5)

Drawn by Carsen Taite. Will the clues lead Detective Claire Hanlon to the killer terrorizing Dallas, or will she merely lose her heart to person of interest, urban artist Riley Flynn? (978-1-63555-644-5)

Every Summer Day by Lee Patton. Meant to celebrate every summer day, Luke's journal instead chronicles a love affair as fast-moving and possibly as fatal as his brother's brain tumor. (978-1-63555-706-0)

Lucky by Kris Bryant. Was Serena Evans's luck really about winning the lottery, or is she about to get even luckier in love? (978-1-63555-510-3)

The Last Days of Autumn by Donna K. Ford. Autumn and Caroline question the fairness of life, the cruelty of loss, and what it means to love as they navigate the complicated minefield of relationships, grief, and life-altering illness. (978-1-63555-672-8)

Three Alarm Response by Erin Dutton. In the midst of tragedy, can these first responders find love and healing? Three stories of courage, bravery, and passion. (978-1-63555-592-9)

Veterinary Partner by Nancy Wheelton. Callie and Lauren are determined to keep their hearts safe but find that taking a chance on love is the safest option of all. (978-1-63555-666-7)

Everyday People by Louis Barr. When film star Diana Danning hires private eye Clint Steele to find her son, Clint turns to his former West Point barracks mate, and ex-buddy with benefits, Mars Hauser to lend his cyber espionage and digital black ops skills to the case. (978-1-63555-698-8)

Forging a Desire Line by Mary P. Burns. When Charley's ex-wife, Tricia, is diagnosed with inoperable cancer, the private duty nurse Tricia hires turns out to be the handsome and aloof Joanna, who ignites something inside Charley she isn't ready to face. (978-1-63555-665-0)

Love on the Night Shift by Radclyffe. Between ruling the night shift in the ER at the Rivers and raising her teenage daughter, Blaise Richilieu has all the drama she needs in her life, until a dashing young attending appears on the scene and relentlessly pursues her. (978-1-63555-668-1)

Olivia's Awakening by Ronica Black. When the daring and dangerously gorgeous Eve Monroe is hired to get Olivia Savage into shape, a fierce passion ignites, causing both to question everything they've ever known about love. (978-1-63555-613-1)

The Duchess and the Dreamer by Jenny Frame. Clementine Fitzroy has lost her faith and love of life. Can dreamer Evan Fox make her believe in life and dream again? (978-1-63555-601-8)

The Road Home by Erin Zak. Hollywood actress Gwendolyn Carter is about to discover that losing someone you love sometimes means gaining someone to fall for. (978-1-63555-633-9)

Waiting for You by Elle Spencer. When passionate past-life lovers meet again in the present day, one remembers it vividly and the other isn't so sure. (978-1-63555-635-3)

While My Heart Beats by Erin McKenzie. Can a love born amidst the horrors of the Great War survive? (978-1-63555-589-9)